BUNGLED

A RYLIE COOPER MYSTERY

STELLA BIXBY

FERRY TAIL PUBLISHING LLC

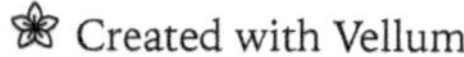 Created with Vellum

It was too early to be awake and much too early to be on a boat checking fishing licenses. But George had been eager to get out.

I wiped the dew off the steering wheel and navigated through the fog. The reservoir was quiet, save a handful of boats and the low grumble of our motor. Every once in a while, we heard the excitement of someone catching a big fish through the fog. Outbursts of excitement were far better than screams of terror.

My uniform was a tiny bit loose on me since I'd dropped a few pounds for my upcoming wedding. I took a sip of my fat-free flavorless coffee and winced. It tasted like tar with a bit of watery milk stirred in, but it would warm me up and force my mind to function so early in the morning—both of which I desperately needed.

"We should check on those guys with the big bass boat," George said. "The ones who launched first."

George was a retired Prairie City cop who decided on a whim to become a summer park ranger, aka a summie. If anyone thought *I* was looking for trouble, they hadn't met George. He thought practically everyone was breaking the law.

He also thought getting on the boat before my second cup of coffee was the best way to catch those supposed criminals.

George could have driven the boat, but he didn't want to, and I was happy to be behind the wheel. When I'd first started as a summie, I'd been horrible at maneuvering the boat. Now, as a full-timer with hours of boat experience, it was one of my favorite parts of the job.

"I think they're over there, in the cove." He squinted against the rising sun.

The surrounding fog shimmered in the brightening light.

Sure enough, the boat we were looking for was back in the cove. I turned in that direction and accelerated slightly.

"What are they doing?" George said, perched on the bow. "It looks like they're dumping something overboard."

"They're probably releasing a fish," I said. "No big deal."

Carmen—the front office manager—was right when she said this year's summies were a bit . . . different. Initially, I thought Ursula hired them to watch me so I'd stay out of trouble. But when that plan blew up like a firework on the Fourth of July, I figured they'd back off and chill out a bit.

Nope.

If anything, they'd gotten worse.

George acted like a paranoid old grandpa who constantly needed to yell at kids to get off his lawn. Tatiana—the retired Florida park ranger—made it seem like she was out to find another alligator to wrestle. And Sondra still hadn't given a single stitch of personal information to any of the full-time rangers but had written more tickets than any summie in the park's history.

I never thought I'd say it at the beginning of summer, but Victoria was the only normal one. Other than following me around like a puppy waiting on me hand and foot while I had a cast on my broken arm, she showed the most potential. Thankfully, since I'd gotten my cast off, she'd taken to following Nikki around instead. I had no doubt Ursula Vilago—the Director of Prairie City's Parks and Recreation Department and Victoria's aunt—had a great deal to do with that after I explained how her niece was driving me crazy.

If only I'd known how much worse it could get. Now, I was stuck working with George—the man who currently looked like he might dive into the water and swim to the fishermen's boat if I didn't hurry and get there.

I eased the throttle forward, forcing him to take a step back so he didn't fall. At least he didn't look like a tiger ready to pounce anymore.

"Hey guys," I said before George could. "How's it going?"

Three fishermen we'd affectionately dubbed the three amigos looked up with big smiles on their faces. These guys wouldn't cause any trouble.

"I didn't expect to see you out here," I said. "What's the occasion?" Usually, they stuck to an inner-city pond, but here they were on Alder Ridge Reservoir in what looked like a brand-new fishing boat.

"Hey, Rylie," Luther said in his deep crackly voice, his eyepatch rising with his smile. "We're getting ready for the big tournament. If the fishing is as good as it is today, we'll win the tourney for sure."

"You should have seen the one we just released," Tom said, hobbling to the side of the boat to hand me his fishing license. "It was massive."

"I have a picture," Ray said, standing a head over the other two, his full white beard twitching as he talked. He pulled out his phone and showed us a picture of a giant walleye.

If it looked big in Ray's hands, it must have been massive.

"Impressive," I said.

"If only we could have caught it next week at the tournament," Luther said.

"There will be more," Tom said. "It's just good to know there are still fish that size in this reservoir. I haven't heard of a big catch since ol' Ronnie got his."

"He got his all right," Ray said with a laugh.

The other two glared at him, and he stopped.

Ronnie had been the first dead body I'd come across as a park ranger. Someone didn't like that he'd caught the state record catfish and did something about it. They also wanted to do something about me. I still shivered when I saw a piece of rope like the one I'd nearly been strangled with.

"Can we see your fishing licenses?" George asked in his cop voice, shutting down all small talk.

Luther and Ray handed him their licenses, giving me sideways glances.

I shrugged.

"When'd you get this awesome boat?" I asked, trying to break the tension. "It's quite the upgrade from shore fishing."

"We all pitched in," Tom said. "We don't get a ton in retirement, but between the three of us, we could afford it."

George handed them their licenses back, and I handed Tom his.

"Now that you know we're legal—" Ray glanced at George, who stood with his arms crossed over his chest and a grumpy look on his face "—I need to tell you about the scuttlebutt."

"I love some good scuttlebutt." I leaned in. Fishermen always had gossip to share.

"Word on the street is some out-of-towners are looking to cash in on the tournament prizes," Ray said.

"Why is that a problem?" George spoke up. "I would imagine fishermen from all over will come out since the prize is worth ten grand."

Ray glared at him. "You didn't let me finish."

George glared right back. The other two men in the boat tried not to laugh at the exchange. Of all the three amigos, Ray was the grumbliest. He was the perfect match for George.

"These out-of-towners have plans to win one way or another," Ray continued.

"Are you saying they plan on cheating?" I asked.

"Just some scuttlebutt." Ray shrugged. "But I'd keep an eye out for anything fishy."

The other two snickered at the fish pun.

"I'll make sure to pass the information along to the event director," I said. "We'll let you get back to it."

When we were out of earshot, George came to stand next to me at the center console. "I still think they're up to something."

I held in a groan. "Not everyone is up to something."

"You'd be surprised," he said. "One can never be too prepared. Do you know how to get out of restraints if someone tries to tie you up?"

I sighed. He'd been trying to teach me little tips and tricks since we'd started working together. "Maybe I'd use my teeth?"

He looked at me like I'd told him I might use a chainsaw. "Your teeth? To break a zip tie?"

"I have strong teeth?" I laughed, but he didn't join. I stopped laughing. "Okay, how?"

He almost smiled. That was about as animated as he got—an almost-smile. "If they zip-tie your hands together behind you, get them in front of you by shimmying them down your butt and then pulling your legs through."

Just the thought of doing that gave me a cramp. How flexible did he think I was?

"Then, once they're in front of you, tighten the zip tie."

"Tighten it?" I laughed again.

He didn't laugh . . . again. "If it's loose, it won't break as easily."

"Tighten it," I said in my most serious voice. "Got it."

"Then you lift it above your head." He demonstrated. "And pull it down across your stomach or side in one big swoop. The force will pop it right off."

"Cool, thanks."

"We could practice when we get back on shore."

"You want to zip-tie my hands behind my back?" That didn't sound fun at all.

"I don't want to," he said. "But it'll help you learn."

"I really don't think anyone will ever zip-tie my hands together."

He looked at me skeptically. "Says the shit magnet."

"I know, I've gotten myself in predicaments before, but—"

"You had a broken arm because some crazy woman attacked you."

"She had a personal vendetta against me," I said. "She was my ex's girlfriend."

"Right, but what if she had zip-tied you?"

"I guess it's a good thing she didn't," I said. "But thank you for the lesson."

"I can teach you more. Like how to get out of a trunk or handcuffs." He looked out across the lake. "You wouldn't believe the things I saw during my time as an officer."

"I was a firefighter at one point," I said. "I've seen some pretty crazy stuff too."

I thought I heard him mutter something about being a *volunteer* firefighter under his breath as he walked to the back of the boat.

I sighed and turned the boat toward the dock. I needed more coffee.

But when we got back to the dock, I forgot all about coffee.

A crowd had formed in the boat trailer parking lot, gathered around one particular boat still on its trailer.

"What the hell is going on over there?" George asked.

"I guess we should go find out." I had hoped I could send him on patrol around the reservoir while I holed up in the office with a cup of coffee and some conversation with Carmen.

Apparently, that wasn't going to happen.

George approached the scene as if he was about to break up a rave. He had his hand on his pepper spray, probably like he would have on his gun when he was an officer.

At first, I thought the crowd of men was oohing and ahhing over a rather spectacular boat. But as I pushed my way through them, I found something even prettier than the state-of-the-art fishing boat.

A woman.

In a bikini.

Holding a massive fish.

No wonder there was a crowd.

I pulled my jacket around me as if trying to fend off the cold she must have been feeling. It wasn't like it was a balmy ninety degrees. I'd be surprised if the temperature was over forty.

But she smiled for her adoring fans and the cameras.

Cameras?

As I looked closer, the scene became clearer.

She wasn't smiling for the men surrounding the boat. She was smiling directly into a video camera lens. And all the while, a woman with a headpiece barked orders to the cameramen and the woman in a bikini.

"What the hell is going on?" I said to no one.

"Don't you know who that is?" Logan—a sports reporter and friend—asked, coming up next to me. She had on a hoodie and jeans and held up a camera of her own, filming not only the woman with the fish, but the entire scene.

"Can't say I do," I said.

"She's a fishing celebrity," Logan didn't look the slightest bit impressed at the sight before her. "Molly Mallard. She's all the rage right now."

"I can see why." It was impossible not to. She had a perfect body—silky brown hair with a slight curl, a cute button nose, huge boobs.

"Women shouldn't objectify themselves for attention," Logan said. "And Molly shouldn't need to. She has serious skills."

She was much more of a feminist than I. She'd actually gotten benched from her job as an NFL reporter for saying some accusatory and damning—yet accurate—things about one of the coaches on live tv when she hadn't known her mic was on. So now she covered random events. Like fishing tournaments, apparently.

"And cut," the woman with the headset said. "That was good, Molly."

Molly smiled, gave the fish a tiny kiss, which made all the men laugh, then eased it down into the live well of the boat.

A man who had been standing off to the side so as not to be in the camera shot wrapped a big jacket over Molly's shoulders.

She smiled up at him—their connection obvious when both of their faces lit up.

"Too bad for these guys, she's already taken," I said.

Logan frowned. "She's actually recently divorced." She looked away, but I caught a blush on her cheeks before she did. "Not that I watched the show or anything."

"What show?"

"It was a fishing show," she said, then hesitated. "But it was more than that. It was like a day in the life type show with her and her husband—now ex-husband."

"Like the Kardashians?"

"I suppose so, only with fishing."

"Sounds stupid," George said next to me. I'd almost forgotten he was there. "I'm going to go patrol if you don't need my help with this spectacle?"

"Go right ahead," I said. Maybe I would get that coffee chat after all.

"Got yourself a live one there," Logan said with a laugh when George was out of earshot.

"He's a gem." I sighed. "Just this morning, he taught me how to free myself if someone zip-ties my hands behind my back."

"Wow," she said. "You should show me sometime."

"I've never actually done it." I laughed. "We could learn together."

"We could make it a date night," she said. "I'm sure Eli wouldn't mind learning. Though he could probably flex, and the zip tie would pop right off."

Eli Hudson was the quarterback for the Denver Broncos and Logan's boyfriend.

"I don't know if Garrett would enjoy that," I said. "He gets pretty antsy about me being in danger."

"For good reason," Logan said. "You're always getting yourself into sticky situations. How's the arm?"

"It's like brand new." I looked back at the dissipating crowd. "Why do you think Molly's here?"

"She's here for the fishing tournament," Logan said. "I'm guessing Ursula had something to do with it." She motioned to where Ursula Villago—the Parks and Recreation Director—stood talking to the woman with the headset.

"Ursula is always trying to do things to get the parks more visibility," I said. "I guess it's not all bad. Is she any good at fishing?" I motioned toward Molly.

"She's fantastic," Logan said. "One of the best fishermen I've ever seen. But her ex-husband always took the spotlight. And since they've broken up, he's won every single competition they've both entered."

"Is he better than she is?"

"That's debatable," Logan said. "I mean, he has won all those competitions, but she has more skill, and you can tell she loves the sport."

"Interesting," I said. "Were you assigned to this one, or was it a choice?"

"Assignment." She sighed. "Eventually, they'll let me back in the NFL. But for now, I'm doing okay."

At least she had a positive attitude about it.

"I probably better go talk to Ursula," I said.

"Don't forget about the zip tie lesson," she said, refocusing her camera. "I seriously want to learn."

I shook my head. I guess I'd have to learn how to free myself from zip ties after all.

"Rylie," Ursula said when she saw me approach.

Molly had climbed down from the boat and was talking to the woman with the headset.

"I'm so glad you came over," Ursula said.

Even when she said she was glad about something, the look on her face said differently.

"I'd like you to meet Molly Mallard," she said.

Molly glanced over at the sound of her name and gave me a sweet smile.

I stuck out a hand. "Rylie Cooper."

"It's nice to meet you," Molly said. "This is a beautiful reservoir."

Ursula beamed. "We're just happy you came out to see it for yourself."

Ursula would do almost anything to bring publicity to her parks. Which probably made her one of the best parks and recreation directors we could have. It also made her a massive pain in the ass sometimes.

"I'm looking forward to competing in the tournament," she said. "Though I hear there's some pretty stiff competition." She glanced over at the group of men still huddled around.

If I had to guess, the competition wasn't the only stiff thing.

"Did you catch that fish you were holding up here?" I asked.

"Sure did." She smiled, then leaned in closer and brought her voice to a whisper. "But I caught it yesterday, incognito."

The man who had handed her the jacket came to stand next to her. His hand brushed hers, and her fingers twitched like she wanted to grab his hand, but then she looked around at the men still gawking at her and shoved her hand into the pocket of her jacket.

"Don't worry," the man next to her said. "Molly will catch one even bigger for the tournament."

Molly smiled. "If there's one thing I'm good at, it's fishing." She shrugged.

"I'm Wanda," the woman with the headset said. "I'm the producer for Molly's show—Fishing with Molly."

"It used to be Fishing with the Mallards," Ursula said. "But Molly and Jess divorced several months ago."

Molly grimaced at the word divorce.

"Molly should have had her own show from the get-go," the man next to her said. "She's the real fisherman. Jess was just along for the ride."

She looked up at him and smiled.

"Gabe's right," Wanda said. "Unfortunately, men get a great deal more respect in this industry. But Molly's making a name for herself. Over the past year and a half, she's become a celebrity in her own right, and her show is currently out-ranking Jess's."

Molly looked uncomfortable with this information being shared.

"Either way," Ursula said. "We're delighted to have you here. I've made arrangements for your accommodations, and Nikki—our event planner—will be here shortly to discuss the event-day logistics."

Nikki would not be thrilled to know Ursula simply referred to her as an event planner. She was also a ranger. And a good one at that.

"It was nice meeting you, Rylie," Molly said. "Maybe you can join us for the logistics meeting?"

I frowned. Why would she want me there? Was she trying to make sure they didn't leave me out of the loop?

"I don't need—"

"Rylie would love to," Ursula interrupted. "We'll see you in the banquet hall around ten." She nodded in a way that said this was not merely a request.

"Sounds like a plan," I said. "I'll see you at ten."

Molly smiled, her slightly crooked, incredibly white teeth shining at me.

When I got to the office, Carmen handed me a cup from Starbucks.

"What's this?" I asked.

"I thought you might need a little something extra after working with George this morning." Her bubbly personality was one of the things I loved most about Carmen. That and how she didn't take anyone's crap. "That guy gives me the creeps."

"He's trying to re-live his glory days as a young police officer," I said, then took a sip of the creamy latte deliciousness. "Ooh, this is definitely not nonfat."

"Non-fat?" Carmen looked at me, puzzled. "Since when do you drink nonfat?"

"I need to be able to fit in my wedding dress."

"You found a dress?" Carmen asked, her eyes lighting up.

"Not yet," I said. "But when I do, I want to be as thin as I can be." I looked at the cup of liquid happiness in my hand.

"Don't you dare waste that," Carmen said as if she'd read my mind. "You are the last person on this planet that needs to lose weight. Now drink up, Buttercup."

I laughed and took another sip. Okay, just this one coffee, then I was back to nonfat plain lattes.

"You know, a wedding dress is only a dress," Carmen said. "When I got married, I bought something at Walmart before we went to the chapel."

"You bought your dress at Walmart?"

"It wasn't a dress," she said. "It was a skirt and tank top. But it seemed fitting for a Vegas wedding."

"You eloped?"

"I met him in Vegas, and we got married." She shrugged. "We're still together all these years later."

I didn't mention the fact that she'd cheated on him with one of our regular fishermen.

"Either way," she said. "The dress doesn't matter. The wedding doesn't matter. What matters is that you're marrying the person you're meant to spend the rest of your life with."

"Then I guess I'm set," I said. "But you could give the speech about things not mattering to my mom and maybe Garrett too. They're a bit over the top when it comes to the planning stuff."

"Usually, the bride is the crazy one." She gave me a skeptical look. She'd made several comments about how she thought I was making a mistake marrying Garrett.

"I guess I feel a bit like you," I said. "The dress—the wedding—doesn't matter as much as the marriage. There's no reason to be a bridezilla when I know I'm marrying the *perfect* guy for me."

She shrugged, not willing to get into an argument about my future love life again.

"Just as long as I can find a dress without lace," I said. "I'll be good."

"No lace," she said. "I guess that's a start."

"It's a start, but do you know how many dresses there are without lace."

"I'd guess about a million."

"It feels like it." I'd been dress shopping about fifteen times. It was getting old. Maybe there was a bit of bridezilla in me after all.

"Regardless of what you wear, I can't wait to be there. It'll be beautiful up there in the mountains." She smiled. "And you'd be beautiful in a potato sack."

"Let's hope it doesn't come to that," I said, and we both laughed.

"What's going on out there?" She pointed out the window to where Molly was signing autographs for the fishermen huddled around her.

"That's Molly Mallard," I said. "She's a famous—"

"Fisherman." Carmen's eyes widened. "Why is she here?"

"She's competing in the tournament." I took another sip. "Apparently, she's meeting with Nikki in a couple of hours."

"She's amazing," Carmen said. "Especially after everything that happened."

I frowned. "What happened?"

"She married Jess Prater—a minor-league baseball player. He's drop-dead gorgeous, but most people would just like him to drop dead."

"Why?"

"He used her to get famous, took her name, cheated on her, then dumped her on live television." Carmen shook her head. "He's a real dirtbag. But it only made Molly look like even more of a saint. She's one of the nicest pretty girls I've ever known."

I laughed. "You know her?"

Carmen waved a hand in the air. "You know what I mean. I know of her."

"I could introduce you."

Carmen smoothed down her eighties-styled blonde hair, only to have it spring back in all its poufy glory. "Me? Meet Molly Mallard?"

"She seems really nice," I said. "I'm sure she'd love to

meet you."

"I—uh—" Carmen struggled to find the words she was looking for. "Maybe some other time. When I don't look so frumpy."

Carmen never looked frumpy. Today she wore black leggings, a leopard-print top, and matching heels. Her makeup was perfectly in place, and her nails were long and cherry red. There was no part of Carmen that didn't look absolutely glamorous in her own Carmenesque way.

"Hello ladies," Tatiana said, walking through the main office door. "How are you this beautiful morning?"

"Doing good," Carmen said. "Wrestled anything today?"

Tatiana laughed and pushed the braided side of her dark black hair over her shoulder. The other side of her head was shaved. She wore blue eye shadow and what I guessed were long false lashes. "My wrestling days are over. That alligator nearly killed me." She looked at me. "Find any dead bodies lately?"

I forced myself not to roll my eyes. First, George calls me a shit magnet, then Tatiana gives me grief about dead bodies. It wasn't like I went out looking for bodies. They just seemed to find me.

"Nope," I said, taking another drink of my coffee.

"Rylie has more important things on her mind," Carmen said. "Like her wedding."

"How does your fiancé feel about your life being in danger all the time?" Tatiana asked.

I shrugged. "I think he's coming around to it."

"That's good. I was engaged once, and she was not okay with it. It didn't help that one of my stalkers threatened her." She contemplated this for a moment. "I probably would have had to quit to be with her, but she'd already made her decision." She shrugged. "If I'd have done that, I probably never would have met so many new friends here in Colorado."

I wasn't sure how Garrett would take it if he were ever dragged into one of the investigations. Especially a dangerous one.

3

Nikki and Victoria were already in the banquet hall when I showed up. They made quite the team. It was like the two most popular girls from competing schools became best friends but still kind of hated each other. They were the ultimate frenemies.

"Hey," Victoria said with a smile. Her long neck—the reason I used to call her giraffe girl—was accentuated by the fact that she had her bleach-blonde hair up in a tight bun. "We're just waiting for Molly to show up."

"I didn't know you were coming." Nikki tucked a strand of silky auburn hair behind her ear with a perfectly manicured finger.

"Molly invited me," I said. "Probably because she didn't want me to feel left out. But when I tried to back out, Ursula insisted I come."

"Today, we need to make sure Molly's ready for the event and that this isn't just a big publicity stunt," Nikki said. "It will make the fishing tournament a hundred times more complicated having her here."

"I'm sorry," Molly said from the door. "I didn't mean to eavesdrop, but if it's better that I back out of the tournament, I can do that."

Nikki stood, a look of embarrassment crossing her face. "That's not what I meant. I just want to make sure you're aware of the possible logistical problems."

"I'll do whatever you need me to," she said. "I don't want to cause any issues. I just want to fish."

It was refreshing seeing a beautiful woman who actually enjoyed fishing. I'd seen lots of women who acted like they enjoyed fishing to impress their hot fishermen boyfriends when they absolutely couldn't stand worms or fish or being outside.

Ursula and Wanda walked through the door, and Molly turned to look at them.

"Are we ready for the meeting?" Ursula said.

Nikki nodded and motioned for us to sit at the circular table where she had various handouts placed in each spot.

Victoria looked to Nikki for cues on what to do. It was almost humorous to watch her copy Nikki motion for motion. Nikki sat. Victoria sat. Nikki shuffled papers. Victoria shuffled papers.

"Let's start with the event schedule," Nikki said when everyone was situated. "The gates will open at five in the morning. Boats will be able to launch immediately."

Wanda cleared her throat. "Excuse me," she said. "But Molly will need early access. She shouldn't have to sit in line with the rest of the fishermen." Wanda wrinkled her nose when she said the word fishermen as if they were beneath her.

"I'm afraid that won't be possible," Nikki said. "It's likely Molly will catch the largest fish in the competition."

Molly blushed.

"And if she wins after given special treatment," Nikki continued, "we could have a lawsuit on our hands."

"This is bigger than a lawsuit," Wanda said. "It's about Molly's safety."

"If Molly wishes to forfeit her entry into the competition," Nikki said, her voice tense, "she can go to the front of the line."

"No," Molly said. "I want to compete. Isn't that what all of this is about? Proving that I'm just as good as-as . . . other fishermen?"

I was ninety-eight percent sure she was about to say Jess but understood why she wouldn't want to pit herself specifically against an ex.

"You have nothing to prove," Victoria said. Everyone looked over at her. "I just mean to say, you're a fantastic fisherman. Everyone knows that. Jess was a tool and knows nothing about fishing. You taught him everything, and he used that knowledge to bolster his career."

I had no idea Victoria cared so much about fishing. But if I had to guess, she likely cared about the reality television drama more than she cared about the actual fishing aspect.

"She's partially right," Wanda said. "You are better than him. He did use you. But she's wrong about proving yourself. You do have to. And you will. Every single day. Because you're a gorgeous woman who just happens to be a fantastic fisherman."

"Plus," Molly looked down at her nails, "Jess has

beaten me in every single tournament since we broke up." She glanced up at Wanda. "Maybe for this tournament, I could downplay the pretty factor. I like sweats and hoodies more than bikinis. I mean, who fishes in a bikini anyway?"

Wanda sighed. "We've had this conversation. If it wasn't for your looks, you wouldn't have a show at all. It's not fair, but it's true."

Molly nodded, and I thought I noticed a tear in her eye.

"Thousands of women fish. Maybe even as well as you do. But they're not pretty. Trust me. I've seen their tapes. And that's why they're not getting their own shows." She turned to Ursula. "Since Molly's become a big name in fishing, women have come out of the woodwork. But they don't understand. Molly doesn't have a show because she's good at fishing."

Molly cleared her throat.

"I mean, she doesn't have a show because she's *only* good at fishing," Wanda corrected. "Unfortunately, we live in a society that cares about the way people look. Almost to a fault." She glanced around at all of us. "Look at all of you. You're stunning. And I'd guess your looks have given you an advantage in many aspects of your lives."

I couldn't believe she was grouping me with Nikki and Victoria. I mean, sure, I wasn't hideous. But they were practically supermodels. I was more like the girl-next-door-athletic type.

Where I looked like a box in my blue and gray ranger uniform, they looked like TV stars who had their uniforms tailored to hug all their perfect curves. And don't even get me started about their hair and makeup.

"Let's get back to the rules," Molly said, obviously

uncomfortable talking about her looks. "How about I get in line—at the front," she said, trying to appease Wanda. "I can sign some autographs. It'll be good for the show."

"If you want to be at the front of the line, you'll have to line up the day before," Nikki said.

"You want her to spend the night in her truck?" Wanda asked. "That's too much. Maybe we should take our show to another tournament."

"Now, now, now," Ursula said. "Let's think about a reasonable solution."

Nikki crossed her arms over her chest.

"Is there someone who could park your truck and boat at the beginning of the line, stay with it all night, and then we could drive you to it in the morning before the gates open?"

Nikki didn't object, though the way her face was turning red made me think she might.

"I think that would work," Molly said. "Does that work for you?" she asked Wanda.

"That's acceptable," Wanda said.

Nikki sighed. "Rylie, can you bring Molly in that morning? Discreetly?"

I nodded. "I'm sure I can make that happen."

Molly smiled at me. "Thank you."

"Now, let's go over the rules," Nikki said.

"Before we get into that," Wanda said. "We need to address the elephant in the room."

"What elephant?" Nikki asked.

"Jess," Wanda said. "We need to make sure Jess won't be part of this tournament."

Nikki raised her eyebrows as she looked at Ursula.

Ursula cleared her throat. "Unfortunately, we can't make that happen."

Molly shifted in her seat.

"And why not?" Wanda asked.

"First and foremost, we are a city. Funded by taxpayers. We cannot pick and choose who we allow to enter our events. The only people not allowed to enter are employees. Banning him would hurt the integrity of the event."

"Because he's black?" Wanda asked.

Ursula narrowed her eyes. "Because he's another professional fisherman, and it would look like we're trying to fix the competition in favor of Molly."

"It's fine," Molly said. "I doubt he'll enter. He's busy with that new girlfriend of his. I think she has some sort of event this weekend." She shrugged. "But even if he does enter, I'll beat him this time. I can feel it."

Wanda didn't look satisfied with that answer but didn't object.

"Now, let's talk about the rules," Nikki said.

Everyone was on their best behavior the rest of the meeting. At one point, Gabe came in and pulled up a chair next to Molly. I wasn't certain, but I thought they might have been holding hands under the table for a moment.

When the meeting was over, Ursula, Molly, Wanda, and Gabe huddled near the door discussing the filming logistics, leaving Nikki, Victoria, and me at the table.

"You guys up for dress shopping again tomorrow?" I asked both of them. "My mom made a reservation at a new bridal boutique."

"Uh well," Victoria said, shuffling the papers in front

of her. "I think I'm busy with—uh—my aunt has this thing. I wish I could, but . . ."

"You don't have to make excuses, Victoria," Nikki said. "No, Rylie. We don't want to go. The first time was fun. The second time was bearable. The third, fourth, and fifth times were ridiculous. You've tried on more than a hundred dresses—I've counted—and none were *the one*."

"I think this time might be better," I said. "I saw a picture on the website of a dress that looked beautiful."

"I'm sure there will be something wrong with it," Nikki said, not even trying to hide her exasperation. "It'll be too long, too short, too revealing, too glossy, too much lace."

"I hate lace," I said.

"That's just the thing," Nikki said. "You hate all of them for one reason or another. Don't you think that might be a red flag?"

"Don't listen to her," Victoria said. "You and Garrett are a wonderful couple, and you deserve to have the exact perfect dress for your wedding. Even if you have to try on a thousand dresses."

Nikki threw her hands in the air. "I don't understand why there's so much pressure to find the perfect dress. It's a dress you'll wear once. One time. And they're so expensive."

She was right, in the practical sense of things.

"No, no, no," Victoria said. "You might wear it once, but it'll live on in pictures the rest of your life. Your children will look at your dress and imagine themselves walking down the aisle. Heck, they might even choose to wear it themselves. It could become a family heirloom."

Victoria looked at Nikki as if she might stick out her tongue. "On second thought, I think my schedule cleared up. I'll be there." She raised her eyebrows when she looked at Nikki.

"Fine," Nikki said. "I'll go too. But this is the last time."

"Did I hear someone say something about wedding dress shopping?" Wanda said, peeking over at us.

I smiled. "I'm having a hard time figuring out what I want to wear."

"Molly is a pro at wedding dress shopping," Wanda said. "Maybe she could join you?"

Molly gaped at her. "I—uh—"

"Come on," Wanda said. "You even said yourself you needed to make some new friends. And wedding dress shopping would be the perfect way to prove you're past the divorce."

"I don't know," I said. "Would there be cameras involved?"

"Not on you," Wanda said. "Maybe a small moment for Molly. It would make great filler for the show. And it'll make Jess crazy."

Molly glanced at Gabe, who was studying the floor.

"I'll go. But not to make Jess crazy," she added quickly. "I don't care what Jess thinks. But it could be fun."

Her tone of voice made it sound like she was signing up for a root canal.

"Can you pick me up?" Molly said to me. "I don't have my own vehicle."

"But that truck—" I said.

"It's Gabe's," she said. "I don't need a vehicle since I'm

always escorted around. But if I don't have to take a hired car, I'd rather not."

"I can pick you up," I said.

"I'll tell you where she's staying," Nikki said. "But this time, you better pick a dress, or I'm not coming again."

Victoria laughed. "Yes, you will. We both will. We're here for you, Rylie."

I smiled. They were some of the best frenemies I'd ever had.

4

M olly's hotel was one of the swankiest and most exclusive in Denver. Part of me wondered if Prairie City taxpayers were paying for her accommodations. Then I laughed because that was something my dad would ask.

After getting through the security gate, I parked out front and waited for Molly to emerge from the large sliding glass doors.

It didn't take long for the action to start. First, Wanda stormed outside, pulling a gorgeous man behind her. If I had to guess, that would be Jess. And Wanda did not seem happy with him.

When she started yelling, I cracked my window to hear what they were saying.

She yelled something about them being divorced.

He pulled off a bright orange hat and held it to his chest as he seemed to be trying to calm her down, but she wasn't having it. She started screaming about ruining production, and if he cared so much, he'd cancel his show.

But it wasn't until Molly walked out that I felt the need to insert myself.

She walked through the doors looking like a normal—yet beautiful—woman wearing ripped jeans, white sneakers, and an oversized gray hoodie. Until she saw Jess. Then she looked like she might pass out. Or cry.

Wanda was still yelling, but her back was to Molly.

Jess's back was to me, but when he saw Molly, his shoulders drooped.

Molly turned to walk back inside, but I stepped out of the car. "Hey, Molly," I said, waving over at her. "Ready to go?"

Wanda whipped around when she heard me call out to Molly.

Molly tore her gaze from Jess and saw me. Her face brightened into a smile.

She said something to Wanda as she walked past without another glance toward Jess.

"I'm so glad you're here," she said, sliding into Cherry Anne's passenger seat. "Nice ride."

"It was a gift," I said. "Sort of." A few months before, a woman trying to warn me off her case had destroyed the original Cherry Anne. In the end, she bought me a brand-new Mustang. "Was that Jess?"

She nodded and watched Jess and Wanda talking a bit more civilly as we pulled out of the parking lot. "I didn't know he was here," she said. "But his producer called Wanda last night and told her he's joining the fishing tournament too."

"That's . . ."

"Fine," she said. "It's fine. He's done this with every event I've entered since our divorce was finalized."

"Why?"

"He's using it to get ratings. His producer tries to create drama between the two of us. They turn even the slightest sideways glance into a big deal." She sighed. "And every time he wins, his ratings spike and mine tank."

"I'm sorry."

"It's okay," she said. "I try to tell Wanda not to worry about it so much, but she just can't get over it. She's way too focused on beating their ratings." She picked at the frays on her jeans. "It probably doesn't help that his producer is her ex."

I laughed. "Sounds complicated."

"It used to be so great," she said, her voice deepening a bit with emotion. "We would double date. The show got fantastic ratings. It was the best time of my life."

"Do you mind me asking what happened?"

"You don't know?"

"I don't watch much TV."

"He cheated," she said. "With the girl he's with now. She's a professional wrestler. Bombastic Becca."

"I'm sorry," I said. "I'm sure that sucked."

"It did," she said. "But I think what hurt the worst was how much it felt like he was simply using me to get famous. I should have noticed. Especially when he pushed to make the TV show and only proposed after we got it. On live TV."

Ouch.

"And I was stupid enough to think we would have kids. Grow old together." Tears were pooling in her eyes, but she quickly swiped them away. "I'm sorry. I don't usually let it get to me."

"It's okay," I said. "I understand cheating exes. I had one myself. My ex's girlfriend tried to kill me not too long ago."

She looked over at me, horrified.

"I'm okay, though," I said. "She just broke my arm. And now they're both in jail."

"Okay, you win," Molly said with a small laugh.

Ugh. Overshare. "Sorry," I said. "I don't know why I told you that."

"It's okay," she said. "I'm sure Jess's new girlfriend wouldn't hesitate to take a shot at me."

"I don't understand it," I said. "They got the guy."

"Yeah." She looked down at her jeans again like she wanted to say more but stopped herself.

"I think this is the place," I said, pulling into a pretty little strip mall.

"It sounded like you've done this a few times," Molly said.

"More than a few," I said. "It's becoming a problem. I just can't seem to find the right dress."

"I had the same issue," she said. "I looked for the better part of six months before Jess had someone make me a dress to my exact specifications."

"That sounds nice," I said.

"It would have been, but I'm not a designer. And if I'd have known what kind of dress I wanted, I would have chosen one. The dress I ended up designing looked like it belonged on the cover of a Halloween magazine. It was hideous." She looked out the window. "Jess was sweet about it. Said it looked perfect. But I couldn't wait to get rid of that stupid thing."

"What did you do with it?"

"I gave it back to the designer," she said. "He said he would recreate it and display the original in his boutique as the most expensive dress he'd ever created. It's a good thing the network paid for our entire wedding."

My parents were paying for my wedding. Garrett had offered to pay for nearly everything, but my parents refused. They spent a fortune on my sister's wedding and had every intention of spending a fortune on mine too.

"Are you sure you're okay doing this?" I asked. "You don't have to shop for dresses with me. I can just tell Wanda that you were here."

"Sure," she said. "I don't know why I'm getting all down in the dumps about Jess. He might be seeing someone else, but so am I."

"Gabe?"

She looked at me like I'd just revealed one of her biggest secrets. "How did you know?"

"Good guess?" I said. "Why? Is it a secret?"

She sighed. "It shouldn't be," she said. "Gabe and I have been friends for a long time. Since we were kids, actually. This was only the next step, I guess."

"Why don't you just tell everyone you're together?"

"The network wants me to be single. It helps with ratings." She shrugged. "Plus, Jess always suspected me of cheating with Gabe." She looked out the window. "I never did. But if he finds out we're together now, I can only imagine the drama he and his producer would concoct."

"I'm sorry," I said. "It must be hard dealing with all of that."

She shrugged. "I guess that's what I get for being famous." She gave me the same smile she'd had when the fishermen surrounded her, then let it drop into a more sincere version. "Let's go inside. I'm sure everyone is waiting for the bride."

She was right. Everyone was waiting. When Carmen saw Molly walk through the doors behind me, I thought she might faint.

"Carmen is one of your biggest fans," I said, introducing them. When I found out Molly was going to come, I knew I had to invite Carmen.

"It's a pleasure to meet you," Molly said, opening her arms for a hug.

Carmen took her up on the offer, and they hugged until they were both giggling.

"Oh good, the bride's here," a man walked into the room wearing multi-colored bell-bottoms and a tight white shirt.

Nikki and Victoria had already gone off to look through the racks.

"Geoffrey," my mom said. "I'm so happy you could fit us in."

"Anything for the woman who bakes the best lasagna this side of the Mississippi."

He hugged my mom. "Should we get this party started?" At the clap of his hands, a tall woman appeared balancing a tray of champagne flutes.

Nikki, Victoria, and Shayla accepted their glasses and sipped from them. I thought I heard Nikki tell the woman something about it being a long day and to keep the champagne flowing, but I chose to ignore her. Maybe today would be the day I'd find the perfect dress.

"Molly?" the woman said when she saw my new friend.

"Melinda?" Molly said when she caught sight of the woman. "And Geoffrey?"

Geoffrey spun around, leaving my mom in the middle of a sentence about alterations.

Geoffrey, Melinda, and Molly did this weird squeal, hug, and jump sequence, and in that moment, Molly looked the happiest I'd seen her.

"This is the man who designed my wedding gown," Molly said after they'd finished their dance hug.

"Molly hated that damn thing," Geoffrey said. "But it's made me so much money."

"Molly could have worn a brown paper bag, and people would have begged to know what tree he made it from," Melinda said.

"Why don't you try on the Molly first?" Geoffrey said, taking me by the arm and leading me to the dressing room. "It probably won't be your style, but I like to give my brides the full treatment. We can't have you walking out of here without a gown, now can we?" He looked over and winked at my mom, who smiled back.

"Looks like he's got your number," Nikki said from the other side of me.

I nudged her. "I'll find one this time. I know it."

She shrugged. "I was grumpy yesterday. If you don't find your dress, I'll be here next time and the time after that and—well—let's just hope that you find one by then, or you might be walking down the aisle in your jeans."

I laughed. "Why were you grumpy?"

Nikki looked behind us where Carmen, Molly, and Melinda were deep in conversation. "It's not that I don't want Molly in the tournament. It just makes everything a bit more challenging. We've had to beef up security, go over the rules about a hundred times making sure they don't favor a professional fisherman, and now Jess will be there."

"Jess?" Geoffrey said, peeking around me. "Again?"

"Again?" Nikki said.

"His producer has been booking him in all the same events as Molly," I said. "Trying to create drama that's not there."

"For Jess, it's there," Geoffrey said, glancing at Molly, who was still lost in conversation. "He only realized he truly loved Molly the moment he lost her."

This sounded like a soap opera.

"But he's dating someone," I said.

"He's a grass is greener sort," Geoffrey said. "At least he was. I think if Molly gave him another chance, he'd jump right on it. She's a special woman."

"I don't think he'll get that chance," I said, glancing back at Molly.

"Nor does he deserve it," Geoffrey said. "But let's not talk about Molly. Today is your day." He opened a heavy wooden door leading to a huge dressing room already decked out with pre-selected gowns. "Start with that one. I didn't know you'd be bringing Molly, but I always have my brides start with my signature gown. One of these days, someone will buy it because they love it, not because it's the same gown Molly Mallard wore." He winked and closed the door, leaving me in a room filled with what looked like a hundred gowns.

The Molly was worse than I imagined.

It was apparent Molly didn't know what she was doing when she designed it, but it baffled me why anyone else would want to buy it. If she and Jess had stayed together, I could see the dress being an ugly-as-sin symbol of a successful marriage. But what it really looked like was an artistic rendering of a marriage gone horribly wrong.

Either way, I tried it on first, like instructed.

I'd pulled my hair back into a bun—the way I assumed I'd wear it on my wedding day—and put on decidedly more makeup than usual. Why they couldn't make lighting and mirrors more flattering in dressing rooms was beyond me. It didn't make for a great bridal experience. I mean, how was I supposed to find the perfect dress when I didn't even look like my best self?

The signature dress was an even bigger disaster when I put it on. Though it wasn't the prettiest dress, George had created it to flatter Molly's body type—thin with big boobs. Neither of which I was or had. And when you combined my larger-than-zero dress size, my normal-sized boobs swam in the fabric intended for Molly's giant tatas.

I spun around, looking in the mirror. The silky fabric hugged my hips and butt, a more ruched fabric was loose around the waist, and the bust was a padded heart-shaped piece that stuck out so far you could see down to my belly button.

"Uh, I don't think I need to show you this one," I said,

peeking my head out the door. "I don't think I have the right build for it."

"Anything can be altered," Mom said. "Please show us."

There was no way in hell I was wearing this dress on my wedding day. I'd tried on some pretty horrible ones, but this one took the cake. I almost felt bad that Molly had been stuck with it for her own wedding. Even if it had fit her perfectly, it was still pieced together like a car with mismatching doors.

"Oh wow," Nikki said, trying to hold back her laughter when I walked out. "That's something else."

Molly looked horrified.

Even Geoffrey shook his head. "All right," he said. "Onto the next one."

I let out a sigh of relief and practically sprinted back toward the dressing room. And when I say sprinted, I mean shuffled as fast as I could with my legs bound in the mermaid tail of the dress.

I almost made it back inside when I tripped.

The world felt like it was in slow motion. I was falling, but I couldn't catch myself.

My legs wouldn't react.

My arms flailed in the air.

My head hit the mirror with a deafening crack then shatter.

Screams were all I heard before the world went black.

5

When I regained consciousness, two paramedics and all of my friends stood over me. I was lying on a stretcher.

"Don't sit up," one of the paramedics said. "You took a nasty fall."

"You're telling me," I said. My head felt like it might explode. I reached up to the source of the pain to find someone applying pressure to the back of my skull.

"Let's keep our hands down," the other paramedic said. "We're going to need to take you in to get the glass removed and stitch you up."

"Glass?" I looked around to find what looked like a crime scene. Blood covered the remains of a broken mirror —its pieces scattered all over the surrounding ground. "Oh no, the dress." I looked down. Thankfully, someone had removed the dress and covered me with a blanket.

"Don't worry, sweetie," Geoffrey said. "I saved it." He motioned to where the hideous white mess hung in its pristine condition.

I sighed a sigh of relief. I didn't know how much it cost, but I didn't want to spend my entire wedding budget on a dress I'd never wear just because I'd gotten blood on it.

"You can either go by ambulance, or someone can drive you as long as they keep pressure on your head," one of the paramedics said.

"No, no," Mom said. "She's going by ambulance. What if the glass lodges in her brain? Or she bleeds out? Nope."

I didn't have the heart to tell her that my skull would likely protect my brain from the glass.

As the paramedics wheeled me out of the boutique—my friends and family following behind—Geoffrey called out, "Let's schedule another time to try on the other dresses. I just know you'll find one you like."

"I'm so sorry," Molly said from beside me. "I should have warned you that dress is cursed."

"Cursed?" I asked.

"I feel terrible," she said. "Geoffrey won't admit it, but every woman who has gotten married in that dress has gotten divorced within the year. None have tried to kill the brides—until now." She gave me a sweet smile. "I hope you'll be okay."

My brain felt fuzzy.

"Only one person can ride with her," the paramedics said.

Everyone looked at each other.

"Can I go?" Shayla asked.

The rest of my friends and family nodded.

Then my mind landed on something. "Does someone have my purse?"

Mom handed it to me. I dug the keys out and handed them to Molly. "You have a license, right?"

"Yes." She smiled. "But you don't have to let me take your car."

"Take it out, go for coffee, whatever," I said. "You deserve a little time to yourself. There's a hat and sunglasses in the center console if you want to disguise yourself."

She hesitantly took the keys from me. "Thanks," she said. "I'll take good care of her."

Shayla climbed into the ambulance and sat next to me.

When they closed the doors, she sighed. "Only you would fall and smash your head while trying on wedding dresses."

"That dress was a death trap," I said with a laugh. "And apparently, it's cursed too."

"You don't need any more bad luck with dresses." Shayla fidgeted with one of her blonde curls. "You know, some people would take this as a sign."

"What kind of sign?" I snapped, then instantly felt bad. "Sorry, I didn't mean to say it like that."

"It's okay," Shayla said. "I just mean things haven't been easy with this whole picking a wedding dress thing. Maybe it's your subconscious telling you that you don't want to get married." She held up a hand, stopping my retort. "And before you say you're ready, stop. Think about it. Just because you might not be ready now doesn't mean you won't ever be."

I didn't have to think about it. Garrett was the one for me. It didn't matter what dress I wore. "I'm ready," I said.

"I don't think my inability to find a dress means I'm not ready. I love Garrett."

"I know you do," Shayla said. "And I'm not one to talk. I don't know what it feels like to be ready."

I raised an eyebrow. "Really?"

She blushed. She'd been dating one of my colleagues—Seamus—for a few months, and they had a trip planned to Ireland the weekend after my wedding. "I mean, I guess I kind of know. Maybe. We don't even know if he'll propose," she said. "But this isn't about me. If you think you're ready, I do too."

I felt like I had a sinking pit in my stomach. But who didn't get a little jittery when it came to getting married? It was a huge commitment. And it would all work out.

The nurse practitioner removed the glass and stitched me up as good as new. The only problem was, they had to shave small parts of my hair to get to the wounds. I didn't even want to look in a mirror.

By the look on Garrett's face, though, I must have looked okay because he rushed over to me and kissed me gently. "Are you okay?"

"I'm fine," I said. "I just let my clumsiness show."

He didn't find my joke funny.

"I'm really okay," I said. "I tried on a dress that never would have worked—I don't have the right body type."

"I like your body type," Garrett said, finally cracking a smile. "It's perfect."

I didn't tell him how much weight I needed to lose

before the wedding. It wasn't a ton, but it was enough to get me out the door for a run most mornings.

Shayla had hitched a ride back to our apartment with my mom, who went to get me a change of clothes. I told her I didn't need them, but she didn't listen.

"Nikki said there's a big fishing celebrity entered in the tournament," Garrett said.

"Two of them," I said. "One is Molly Mallard, who seems like one of the nicest, most genuine people I've ever met. And the other is her ex-husband, Jess Mallard. I don't know what kind of vibe I get from him yet."

"I think I've seen that show," Garrett said, a blush spreading up his cheeks. "I watched it when you and I first got together so I could impress you with my fishing knowledge."

"But you already knew how to fish," I said.

He shrugged. "I thought I could learn more. But honestly, that show was more about the drama than the fishing. It pulled me in, but not with a rod and reel."

He laughed at his punny joke. He'd make the perfect dad someday with all those dad jokes.

"Molly seemed nice on the show," Garrett said when he stopped laughing. "I think she's the one who actually liked the fishing."

"She has my car," I said.

"Molly Mallard has your car?" Garrett looked at me like I'd taken a few too many painkillers.

"We met yesterday, and her producers forced her to go dress shopping with me." I tried to sit up a bit in bed. Garrett helped me with the pillows behind my back. "She didn't have a car, so I figured I'd send her home with mine."

"Makes sense," Garrett said.

"Miss Cooper," the doctor said, walking in.

I smiled.

"If you're feeling up to it, you're welcome to leave." He went over the x-rays they'd taken and prescribed some medication that I definitely wouldn't be getting filled. I'd be fine with my trusty Tylenol.

Garrett called my mom and told her to stay at the apartment, but she wasn't there when we arrived. She left a note on the counter that she was picking up dinner and would be back.

"Why doesn't she just text you?" Garrett asked.

"Old habits?" I shrugged. "I think I'll lie down for a while before she brings the food."

Garrett helped me into bed and asked about a dozen times what he could get me before I finally convinced him I didn't need anything. He kissed me on the forehead and eased the door closed.

I reached for my phone out of habit and noticed a text message from an unknown number.

Heard you got attacked by a cursed dress. Haha. Be more careful. Luke.

I read the message twice more before texting back.

. . .

I only hope my hair will grow back quickly.

I waited as long as my eyes would stay open for a reply, but none came.

Luke was overseas training people to be police officers. I rarely heard from him, but he talked to Shayla quite a bit. Between Luke and Troy, my two long-term relationships before Garrett, I'd put myself through the wringer.

Luke was my high school sweetheart, and when he proposed the day of our high school graduation in front of our entire graduating class, I literally ran away and didn't talk to him for years. Then, after five years with Troy, I'd finally gotten used to the idea of marriage. Not that he had been planning on proposing. He was too busy sleeping around.

It was no wonder I had terrible luck with the whole idea of marriage. It wasn't Garrett's fault I was all messed up.

"Oh good, the mean girls aren't here," Seamus—Shayla's boyfriend—said in his distinctly Irish brogue as he walked into the training room at the shop. "And what the hell happened to yer head?"

"The mean girls?" I asked, ignoring his question. I'd practically begged my mom and Garrett to let me come to work, even if my head looked a little swollen and my hair was patchy. It was nothing a loose-fitting hat wouldn't fix. A hat I was now pulling on.

"Niktoria," Dusty replied, trying not to look at my head. He'd recently let his curly black hair grow into a short afro, and it made him look even more model-esque than his previously bald head.

Ben, Antonio, and I burst out laughing.

"Niktoria?" I laughed again.

"You know, Nikki and Victoria?" Dusty explained. "They're practically the same person right now. Completely joined at the hip."

"And mean girls?" I asked.

"They're like the popular girls from high school," Dusty said. "Inseparable, mean, might turn on one another at any moment."

"They're not that bad," I said, then lowered my voice in case the summies came in. "Before the summies get here, I want to make sure everyone keeps an eye out for George. He seems intent on finding himself a criminal even when there isn't one to be found. If he's not careful, he'll draw harassment charges."

"It must be hard going from being a respected police officer to a lowly summie," Antonio said. Even when he wasn't trying, his Italian charm oozed from him like slime through my nephew's fingers.

"That doesn't make it okay for him to harass people," I said. "I'd happily take Victoria back."

"Do you think he'll really get harassment complaints?" Ben asked. He was older than the other rangers and, besides Greg—who had been around since the beginning of the ranger program—was the senior ranger in the room.

"You know the three amigos?" I asked.

Ben nodded.

"He acted like he wanted to arrest them because they were releasing a fish. I thought he might jump onto their boat and start searching for something suspicious."

"Well, you are the shit magnet," Dusty said, his deep voice tinged with laughter. "He probably would have found a dead body or severed hand or something."

"Yeah, yeah," I said. "But seriously."

"I'll talk to him," Ben said. "He may have been a police

officer, but he's not exactly equipped to handle the same types of situations with pepper spray."

"You don't think he carries?" Dusty asked.

"He's not supposed to," Ben replied. "Against employee policy."

"He's retired police," Dusty said. "He probably does what he wants."

This gave me a small sense of peace. I never wanted to carry a gun, but that didn't mean I didn't see the value in a trained marksman carrying one. Especially with all the crap that seemed to follow me.

The conversation died when George, Tatiana, and Sondra walked in. They seemed to stick together when they had the chance. Their discussion also died when they noticed we were all silent.

"Hey guys," Ben said in his jolly voice. "How's it going?"

"Park's looking good, boss," Tatiana said.

George sat as far from me as possible.

"How are you, Sondra?" Antonio asked.

"Fine," she said.

Antonio shrugged when he saw my attempt to cover my laugh.

One-word answers were all we usually got from her.

"Good, you're all here," Nikki and Victoria swept into the room like goddesses. "You doing okay, Rylie?"

"Niktoria has arrived," Seamus said under his breath, and everyone laughed.

Nikki turned and glared at us while Victoria looked on.

"I'm fine," I said.

She nodded. "Now, we don't have time for laughter,"

Nikki said. "We have the biggest fishing tournament in the state coming up and two celebrity fishermen attending. Preparation is key."

"We did this for years before it got shut down," Antonio said. "I think we know what we're doing."

"But we're happy to hear what you have to say," Ben added.

"Good," Nikki said, "because I'm changing everything you did in the past."

The room felt like it deflated.

"There's a reason it was canceled—too many prizes, not enough entries." Nikki took a breath. "This year, there will be at least double the highest number of participants with fishermen coming from all over the world."

"The park cannot hold double," Antonio said. "It could barely accommodate the numbers we had in the past."

"We're opening the back field for parking." Nikki stared at him. "Everything will work if you do as I say."

Victoria mimicked Nikki's stance—hands on her hips, feet wide—but she smiled at me when we made eye contact.

Nikki spent the better part of an hour telling everyone what they needed to do during the event. My job was at the weigh-in station.

"Any other questions?" Nikki said.

"Not a question," I said. "But something to look out for."

Nikki nodded for me to go ahead.

"The other day, the three amigos told me they'd heard news about people who plan on cheating."

"How are they planning on cheating?" Nikki asked.

I shrugged. "No idea."

"I was there when the fishermen warned us," George jumped in. "I think they're trying to divert attention off themselves. If anything, we need to keep an eye on those specific fishermen."

I closed my eyes for a couple of seconds and took a deep breath. The three amigos were the last people who would cheat.

"Anything else?" Nikki asked.

The rangers shook their heads.

"Then I'll see you bright and early Saturday morning." Nikki clapped her hands together, and Victoria did the same.

We all stood, and I went to the front to talk to Niktoria.

"How are you?" Victoria asked. "Is your head—"

She reached up to touch it, but I backed away.

"It still hurts," I said. "But they said they got all the glass out."

"Weddings just don't seem to be your thing," Nikki said. "Maybe you and Garrett should elope."

I thought about this for a minute. My parents had paid for everything already. Well, everything besides the dress.

"It's okay," I said. "I just need to find a dress. Preferably one that's not cursed."

Victoria's eyes widened. "That dress was cursed? No wonder you nearly died smashing your head into a mirror."

"I didn't nearly die," I said.

"Tell that to all the blood you lost," Victoria said, her face turning a shade towards green.

"Head wounds bleed more than regular wounds," Nikki said. "Didn't they teach you that in training?"

Victoria shrugged.

"What should we do about the whole Molly and Jess situation?" I asked.

"What situation?" Nikki asked. "They'll come out and fish. Separately. There will be minimal intersection. Their camera crews have been instructed to stay away from each other. They've done this before. And Jess and Molly aren't speaking to one another anyway, so it shouldn't be a problem."

"What if one wins over the other?" Victoria said.

"One of them probably *will* win," Nikki said. "If I was a betting woman—which I'm not—I'd put my money on Molly. She's amazing and due a win. While you were smashing yourself into her dress and then into the mirror, she was telling us about all her fish stories. If even half of them are true, she's a legend in the making."

"I would bet they were all true," Victoria said. "And I am a betting woman."

Nikki shook her head. "You cannot bet on the tournament. It could be construed as giving favor to one of the contestants."

"How does that work?" I asked. "It's not like her betting on Molly will make the fish Molly catches any bigger."

"Working in the public eye is not about reality. It's about perception," Nikki said. "If someone perceives that we rigged the competition in any way, shape, or form, we could be in for a legal battle, and future events will be canceled."

"Well, I won't formally bet on it," Victoria said, "but Molly has this one in the bag. If you watch Jess's show closely, they cut the very specific parts of actually catching the fish. Anyone could be catching his fish and then handing him the rod so he can reel it in."

We both stared at Victoria. She didn't seem like the type to care about fishing.

"What?" she said. "I wanted to be prepared, so I binged the shows last night."

Nikki looked annoyed but didn't say anything. "After you bring Molly to her truck Saturday morning," Nikki said to me. "Make sure you go down to the plaza to get the weigh-in station set up to the specifications in the book. One of the Colorado Parks and Wildlife guys will meet you there. You'll be working together for the weigh-in."

"Aye aye, captain," I said, giving her a mock salute.

She turned away toward the stairs, then turned back. "Make sure Molly's not late and get her in as discreetly as possible."

"Will do," I said. "And Nikki?"

She raised her eyebrows impatiently. "What?"

"Take a breath," I said. "Everything will be great."

"Says the woman who can't even pick out a wedding gown." Her words would have cut, but the teasing smile on her face softened them. At one time, I would have hated her for that remark, but we'd since become friends. She was even going to be one of my bridesmaids.

Victoria gave me an apologetic smile as the two of them made their way down the spiral staircase.

"You know," Antonio said from behind me, making me

jump. "My sister had a hard time deciding on her wedding dress too."

I put my hands on my hips. Where was he going with this? "And?"

"I think it was too much pressure."

"What did she do?"

"She asked her fiancé what he liked." Antonio smiled. "It seemed to help. She found the dress. But then . . ."

"But then what?"

Antonio waved a hand in the air. "Nothing. I should have kept my mouth closed."

"Tell me. Did he hate it? Did something happen?"

"Her fiancé loved it. Well, he loved the back of it."

"Just the back?"

"That's all he got to see as she was running away." Antonio frowned. "Sorry, that was a terrible example. But really, asking Garrett what he likes might give you a direction to go."

Despite his story, he had a point. I had no idea what Garrett would want.

***

"I have a question for you," I said as Garrett and I sat down for dinner at his house that night. Babbitt and Fizzy —our dogs—lay next to the fireplace, their noses almost touching.

"Ask away," Garrett said. He wore a pair of light jeans that accentuated his muscular thighs and cute butt and a polo that barely fit around his biceps.

"What kind of wedding dress do you picture me wearing?"

Garrett's face lit up. "I was wondering if you'd ask me. Not that you have to wear what I want you to," he added quickly. "But since you're asking."

I didn't think he'd get this excited about what I wore.

"I've always pictured my bride wearing a long white gown. A v-neck." He rolled his eyes skyward as if imagining it in his mind.

A v-neck could work. I'd tried on a couple that were okay.

"But the thing I imagine most is a lace back with buttons."

I nearly choked on my beer. "Lace?"

Garrett nodded enthusiastically. "I think lace is super sexy but also very elegant. You'd look great in lace."

Why had I asked? Now, if I didn't get a lace gown, he'd be crushed. And I really didn't want a lace gown.

"But if that's not what you want, you don't have to."

My mom always said I wore my emotions on my sleeve.

"No, it's okay. I just never really . . . considered lace. That's all." I tipped my beer bottle back and sucked down the rest of its contents.

"Seriously, if that's not what you want, I won't be mad."

He wouldn't be mad. He'd be heartbroken.

"Well, I can't tell you what I'm going to choose because that would ruin the surprise." I flashed what I hoped was a sincere smile. "But I'm glad I asked."

Lies.

So many lies.

But how bad would it be to choose a dress with a lace back? And buttons sounded nice. Especially if it made him happy.

The next time I tried on gowns, I'd go straight to the lace section and try on a couple. Maybe I'd be pleasantly surprised.

7

It was dark when I left my apartment to pick up Molly the morning of the tournament. Something orange poked up through the backseat when I threw my work bag back there. I tugged it out to find a hat. It looked like the same hat Jess had been wearing outside the hotel when he and Wanda had been fighting.

I examined it and found a couple of short curly black hairs stuck in the mesh.

I sighed. Sometimes it was hard getting away from exes, but Molly didn't seem the type to get back together with Jess. Especially not in the backseat of someone else's car. But the way that hat was wedged down there could only be accounted for by a handful of actions. One of them being a hook-up in a vehicle that is in no way associated with you.

I put it on the passenger seat and drove to the hotel.

When Molly opened the door and saw the hat, she looked like she might pass out.

"Good morning," I said. "You ready to win a fishing tournament?"

She picked up the hat and examined it. "Where did you find this?"

"It was in the backseat," I said. "Come on, get in."

"I can't," she said. "I need to—just a second."

She slammed the door and stormed back to the hotel.

I turned the car off and followed her. Nikki put me in charge of getting her there on time, and I couldn't screw it up.

"Where are you going?" I yelled after her, but the valet gave me a dirty look.

She raced up the stairs, not even bothering to take the elevator.

I followed, my heart beating so hard it probably made more noise than my footsteps. What was she doing?

By the time we reached the fourth floor, I realized I needed to work out more. My morning runs just weren't doing it.

She stopped about half-way down the hall and banged on the door.

I glanced around. Her knock could have woken the entire floor. Surely security would show up at any moment.

I stayed back and waited. I wasn't about to be hauled off to jail because some crazy woman was screaming at a door.

Yep.

Now she was screaming.

Though her screams were like those of a fluffy little

bunny, if a fluffy little bunny knew how to scream. They were almost adorable.

The door opened, and a camera poked out. Not like a point-and-shoot camera. A big honking television video camera.

This seemed to have absolutely no effect on Molly's mood. In fact, I thought she might actually punch the cameraman.

But it wasn't the cameraman she was focused on so intently.

It was Jess.

"What the hell is this?" she said, pushing the hat into his chest.

"Where'd you find it?" Jess said. He was not ready for the fishing tournament. He wore boxers, a confused expression, and nothing else.

"You know darn well where I found it, Jess."

His expression deepened. "I really don't." I could feel his panic. Did she think he and I had been together in my backseat?

A woman I assumed was Bombastic Becca appeared at Jess's side wearing a see-through negligee and sleek blue hair. You'd think a professional wrestler would be larger—bulkier—but her muscles were defined and sleek. She easily stood a head taller than Molly, who wasn't giving her the time of day. If Jess had a type, it was big boobs, but that was about all the two women had in common.

"Is that your hat?" Becca asked.

"It looks like my hat," Jess said. "But I don't think it is."

"It has your hair in it," Molly said, pulling out a piece that matched the curls on his head.

"That could be anyone's hair," Jess said, but he was starting to look concerned.

"It's yours, you lying, cheating, dirtbag," Becca said. "I can't believe you were with her after we just—"

"I wasn't with him," Molly interrupted. "I found it in the backseat—"

"The backseat of your car?" Becca asked. She looked murderous.

"Not my car, Rylie's car." She pointed over to me, then looked instantly regretful when the cameraman whipped around and pointed the lens at me.

"Who the hell is she?" Becca asked.

"I've never seen that woman before in my entire life," Jess said, confused.

"Sure you haven't," Becca shouted.

The cameraman turned his focus back to the main event, leaving me with heart palpitations. I needed more caffeine to deal with so much drama so early in the morning.

"Didn't you have Rylie's car for a couple of days, Molly?" the cameraman asked, moving to get the entire shot with all of their expressions.

Becca's rage turned back to Molly.

"I did," she said. "But Jess was never with me in it."

Becca didn't look convinced. "I knew you'd go back to her. All you ever do is talk about her."

Molly gaped at them.

"I love you," Jess said to Becca, and Molly's face fell a bit. "I wasn't with her. I'd never do that to you."

"You did that to her," Becca said. "How do I know you won't do it to me too?"

"You know exactly why," Jess said. "Things are different with us. We're engaged. I actually love you."

Becca crossed her arms over her chest, smashing her enormous boobs upward so they almost touched her chin.

"Stay away from me," Molly said, standing a bit taller. "All of you, or you'll end up on the wrong side of—well—life." She was so sweet, even her death threats sounded cute.

She muttered something to the cameraman as she walked past him toward me.

Jess looked like he might want to call out to her, but he didn't. What good would that do? If he was trying to prove his loyalty to Becca, it would do him no good to tell Molly he actually had loved her.

"Let's go," Molly said, grabbing my arm.

I followed her down the stairs and out to the car. Once inside, she started crying.

I patted her on the shoulder as we headed in the direction of the reservoir. It was a good thing I factored in so much extra time so we weren't late. The last thing I needed was an angry Nikki.

"I'm so sorry about that," Molly said. "I'm sure they'll edit you out of the shot."

"It's okay," I said. "But how in the world did his hat get in my backseat? I swear I've never met him before."

"Howard put it there," she said. "He's the producer who is always trying to start drama."

"So he put Jess's hat in the back of my car?"

"Either it would make it look like I was with him, or

you were," she said, wiping a tear from her face. "I can't believe he wasn't even ready for the tournament. It looked like he'd just woken up."

I sighed. "If he's only coming out for the drama, then he probably doesn't care about catching the biggest fish. I mean, ten thousand dollars really can't be much when it comes to how much you guys make with the television show."

"Every little bit helps." She shrugged. "But you're right about him not caring about the fishing part. He hates fishing." Her eyes widened, and she slapped a hand over her mouth. "Oh my. Please don't tell anyone I told you that. It's in my non-disclosure."

"He made you sign a non-disclosure about how much he hated fishing?" I laughed.

She looked at me with a dead-serious expression. "It was the only way I could keep the show."

"I'm sure you could have started a new show just like he did."

"If only," she said. "Half of the reason people watch my show now is because I fish in a bikini. If I started a show from scratch, that would be the only reason all of them watched."

"How is that?" I asked. "I don't know that I could ever go on camera wearing a bathing suit."

"Why not?" she asked. "You have a great body."

I almost pointed out the extra five pounds around my mid-section and my jiggly thighs but thought better of it. Body positivity and all. "I don't like being in front of a camera either, regardless of what I'm wearing."

"It's not as bad as it sounds," she said. "I grew up in

Florida. I practically went to school in a bathing suit. And I get paid for what I love—fishing. If wearing a bikini is the way to make that happen, then that's what I'll do."

"It'll be cold today," I said. "How do you stay warm?"

"I won't wear one today. The network agreed to let me wear sponsored gear when I'm doing competitions."

"That's good," I said. "I think we have a couple of minutes to spare. Do you want to stop for coffee or anything?"

"Ooh, is that Dunkin?"

Dunkin Donuts was on the corner just ahead. I turned into the parking lot.

"I'll be right out," she said. "What do you want? Don't say nothing. We don't have time for that."

I laughed and gave her my order.

She was in and out in record time. Behind her, a trail of five men carried bags and bags of what looked like donut boxes.

"Are you hungry?" I asked when she opened the door, and the men loaded the donuts into my backseat, then the trunk.

"I have a plan," she said with a cute smile, then turned to the men and handed them each a tip. "Thank you so much."

They looked thrilled.

"Oh, and here's your coffee," she said, handing me one of the two cups. "We better hurry so we're not late."

8

Cars, trucks, boats, and campers lined the main highway and the park entrance road.

"That's a lot of fishermen," Molly said, a bit of nervousness entering her voice.

"You got this," I said. "Don't worry about them. Half are probably just here to meet you."

I drove past them, a few honking as I passed. They probably didn't know I was a park ranger and thought I was some entitled fisherman trying to get to the front of the line.

I glanced over at the woman next to me. They weren't entirely wrong.

Her boat was at the very beginning of the line with an anxious-looking Gabe and Wanda standing next to it. When they saw Cherry Anne, they almost jumped out in front of me. Antonio was in the big black Chevy ranger truck keeping the line of cars from coming in, and he stopped them from walking into the road.

"Can you help me with the donuts when we get out?" Molly asked.

"What are we doing with them?" I glanced back at the boxes of yumminess that had been making my mouth water with their delicious sugary smell since we left Dunkin.

"I want to give them out to the fishermen as they pass," she said.

"But that'll make it so you're the last one in the water," I said. "Doesn't that completely defeat the purpose of Wanda getting you to the front of the line?"

"Wanda won't like it," she said. "She's really set on me winning this thing. But after what happened this morning, I'm going to need some good publicity. Plus, this way, no one can say I was given an unfair advantage when I win."

She was smart.

"I can help you get them out of the car," I said. "But then I have to go down to the plaza and get the weigh-in station set up."

"Deal," she said.

"Where have you been?" Wanda shouted when we stepped out of the car. "I've been calling your cell."

Molly glanced down at her purse. "Sorry, I had a bit of a run-in."

"Please tell me it wasn't with Jess."

Molly looked down at her cute white tennis shoes.

"Howard planted Jess's hat in the back of my car," I said. "To make it look like he was either with Molly or with me. She had every right to confront Jess about it."

"I knew what they were up to the minute I saw the

hat." Molly didn't look up. "I should have just let it go, but I'm so sick of him messing with me."

"We've talked about this," Wanda said. "We have to be the bigger people. Those men are nothing to us anymore."

I snuck a glance at Molly. She was nodding but still seemed hurt by Jess's declaration of love toward Becca.

Gabe looked defeated. It probably didn't feel great to know your secret girlfriend still had feelings for her ex-husband.

"Please tell me they didn't get it on camera," Wanda said, though by the tone of her voice, she already knew the answer.

"They did," Molly said. "But I have an idea to make it better."

She explained her donut theory, and Wanda looked like she might strangle Molly, but eventually, she came around.

"Gabe, will you help me get them out of Rylie's car so she can get to her station?" Molly asked.

I moved to help them, but Wanda stopped me. When Molly and Gabe were on the other side of the car, she said, "For the love of God, tell me you weren't messing around with Jess in the back seat of your car."

I laughed. Then realized she wasn't joking. "No," I said. "No way. I'm engaged. Happily."

"Do you think Molly was?"

I looked over at where she and Gabe seemed to be caught up in a bit of an argument.

"No." I shook my head. "She wasn't. I'm pretty confident Howard planted the hat."

"He's such a trash bag," she said. "Anything for views.

But Molly's too smart for that. Too good."

I didn't want to tell her how Molly had lost her cool on Jess. She'd see it herself, eventually.

"Ten minutes," Antonio called out behind me.

"I need to go," I said.

Wanda stepped out of my way.

When I got to the other side of the car, Molly was whispering to Gabe. "I'm so sorry," she said.

Gabe saw me approach, picked up a few bags from the back of the car, and walked away.

"What are you sorry about?" I asked Molly. "Please tell me you weren't actually with Jess in the back of my car."

Molly sighed. "You can believe whatever you want to believe. Everyone will. That's just how it goes." She lifted a few bags from the trunk. "I'll see you later." She walked away without another word.

"Molly, I didn't mean—"

Wanda stepped in front of me and held out her hands for the bags of donuts I was holding. "Molly likes you. She thinks you're her friend. Don't disappoint her."

The words were a warning. And I had no doubt Wanda had every intention of backing them up. A shiver ran down my spine, and it wasn't from the cold air.

It was still dark when I got to the shop.

Nikki's voice rang out when I clicked on my radio, piercing the silence. "I need traffic control help at the main gates. I have reports people are jumping the line."

Ben's voice responded. "Copy, I'll head that way."

"Thanks, clear," Nikki said.

I clicked the mic on my shoulder and spoke into it. "Ranger Seven, Ranger Six?"

"Six," Nikki said. She may have been stressed, but her voice gave away nothing.

"Just so you are aware, the line of cars has extended out onto the highway as far back as the intersection leading to the interstate."

"Copy," Nikki said. "I have PD coming to assist in traffic control as we speak."

"Clear," I said.

"Oh, and Seven?" Nikki said.

"Go ahead."

"I need you in the plaza ASAP to set up the weigh-in station."

Like I didn't already know that. "Copy, be right there."

"Clear," Nikki said. And then silence.

The sky was so clear you could see a plethora of stars, which was pretty but made the air cold. I pulled on my heavy jacket and took a swig of my nonfat latte. It would be a long day.

I got the weigh-in station set up precisely to Nikki's specifications with plenty of time to spare.

I'd set up in one of the thatched-roof, open-air picnic shelters. Three tables blocked the entrance, and a railing blocked the other three sides. Inside, I set up four tall propane heaters—the kind you'd see at an outdoor wedding—a couple of chairs and an extra table.

The front tables held a scale large enough to weigh a fish much bigger than anything that might be pulled from Alder Ridge Reservoir. A few clipboards with sheets each fisherman had to fill out before we weighed their fish were stacked next to a measuring stick, pens, and a computer. Nikki had tasked the summies with entering all the measurements and contestant information into a spreadsheet.

I checked and double-checked that everything was perfect.

From the sound of things on the radio, the traffic situation was horrid. I could hear a tone of I-told you-so in the guys' voices, but Nikki didn't seem to care.

"Are you Rylie?" a deep voice asked from behind me as I clipped the weigh-in papers to the clipboards.

I swiveled around to find a man in his late forties or early fifties with a uniform that suggested he was a Colorado Parks and Wildlife—or CPW—officer.

"Yep," I said. "You must be Peter."

He smiled, making his bushy mustache twitch upward to show a row of sparkly white teeth.

"It's nice to meet you," he said, shaking my hand. "I'm excited about the tournament this year."

"Have you worked it in the past?"

"I've been working this tournament since the very beginning," he said. "It was such a bummer when they canceled it a few years back."

"I heard it just wasn't making enough money."

"That and some shady dealings were happening." Peter looked around as if someone might have been listening, even though the park was still empty and the other rangers were busy with their assigned jobs. "Back then, there wasn't guaranteed prize money like you have this year."

"So, how did people win?"

"Tagged fish. We—CPW—would tag a bunch of fish and release them the week before the tournament. If someone caught a tagged fish, they'd win one of the prizes. If they caught the tagged fish with the gold tag, they'd win the grand prize."

"Sounds reasonable. But what if no one caught any of the fish? Could make for a relatively boring award ceremony."

"We had that happen a couple of years," he said. "And yeah, it wasn't good. Turnout after those years was dismal. People were starting to think the system was rigged."

"Was it?"

"Of course not," Peter said with a gentle smile. "We even took a video of the fish and releasing them, but then about five years ago, every single tagged fish was caught in one day."

"Wait, how many fish are you talking?"

"That year, there were fifty. And they were all caught, including the one with the gold tag. Meaning the city had to shell out tens of thousands of dollars in prize money."

I couldn't imagine the tournament made that much from entry fees. "That must have been quite the budgetary disaster."

"It was. But what made it worse was that the same thing happened the following year. And the year after that too."

"Wait, so three years in a row, every tagged fish was caught?"

He nodded and took a sip of his coffee. "It was almost as if the tagged fish were jumping into people's boats. It's not like fishing here is the easiest in the world."

Almost every time I talked to a fisherman, they complained about how hard it was to catch fish at Alder Ridge Reservoir. I couldn't believe within a ten-hour time-frame, not only were fifty fish caught, but fifty *specific* fish.

"How did that happen?"

He shrugged. "Eventually, we figured out they were putting identical tags on the fish they caught. Someone had to have given them the tag ID numbers—someone on the inside." He looked around conspiratorially.

"That's crazy," I said. "Did you ever find out who was behind it?"

He shook his head. "But we know that's the case because the fish with the same tag ID numbers have been caught in the years since."

"I guess it's good they changed it to be by weight instead of a tag."

"It definitely is."

"I have heard rumblings about cheating schemes in the works." I took a sip of my latte and winced. I only had to deal with the bitter coffee for a few more weeks.

"I'm sure people have lots of ideas on how to cheat," Peter said. "These things seem to attract cheaters. That's why we have to be super on top of our game today."

He held out a fist for a fist bump. I resisted the urge to blow it up like I did with my nephews.

9

Within seconds of Antonio opening the gates, fishermen had lined the shores, and the boat ramp was jam-packed.

It wasn't but ten minutes after Antonio let everyone in that we had our first weigh-in. People were still trying to launch their boats—yelling profanities that echoed up the boat ramp and through the plaza. Four rangers were on the ramp, trying to keep them from killing one another.

"I know this probably won't win the grand prize, but I think it's pretty big." The man pulled a wiggling large-mouth bass from his cooler and handed it to Peter.

"Fill this out while we weigh it, okay?" I handed him a clipboard, and he scribbled in the details.

Peter laid the fish on the table and expertly checked the length from the tip of the fish's face to the end of its tail before setting it on the scale. "Nine pounds five ounces," Peter said, and Sondra put the number into a spreadsheet.

The man's face lit up as he handed me the clipboard and took the fish back.

"Can I snap a picture, please?" Tatiana asked. It was part of our effort to combat cheating—snapping a photo of all the fish weighed in.

The man held up his nine-plus pound fish and smiled. She snapped the photo, and he quickly put the fish back in the water-filled cooler where it splashed to life. "If you guys are good, I'll go release this guy."

"We're good," Peter said with a smile. "Good luck."

"Thanks, man."

"That was fun," I said.

"It sure is nice to have the extra help up here," Peter said to Tatiana, Sondra, and George.

Tatiana and Sondra each had a specific duty while George roamed as if he were the resident security guard. Which maybe he was. I didn't know what kind of agreement he had with Nikki.

"It looks like things are running smoothly down there," Peter said, motioning toward the boat ramp. "Even if the fishermen sound angry."

I gulped my coffee and watched as the last of the fishermen launched their boats.

"Your rangers have always done a phenomenal job of running this tournament," Peter said. "I've been to tournaments all over the state, and none have been run as professionally as this one."

"I just hope we can keep that professionalism with more than twice the number of participants. Some of the other rangers—the ones who have worked this tournament before—weren't thrilled that we were increasing the size so dramatically."

Peter nodded. "I can imagine. Sometimes less is more. I guess we'll have to wait and see."

Over the radio, I heard chatter about a boat with a gas engine. Alder Ridge Reservoir was primarily a drinking water source, which meant the only boat allowed a gas engine was the ranger boat.

Eventually, Ben came back on and assured everyone it was simply a modified electric engine owned by none other than Jess Mallard.

I laughed. It was no surprise he had some sort of randomly modified boat to give him the upper hand.

And sure enough, not an hour later, he came strutting up holding a massive blue cooler, surrounded by Howard, a cameraman, and about fifteen squealing women.

Howard barked out orders to the cameraman while Jess acted like it was just another day of fishing.

I tried not the let the excitement get to me. But when Howard pulled a monstrous fish from the cooler and handed it to Jess—who looked disgusted to touch it—I could feel my heart rate increase.

I knew in my gut this fish would be the winner.

I hadn't seen many catfished pulled from the reservoir, but when I did, they were massive.

"Bring it on over," Peter said, holding out gloved hands.

Jess looked happy to give Peter the fish, wiping his hands on his pants vigorously when Peter took possession.

The fish flopped a couple of times when Peter lowered it down on the scale.

Everyone held their breath as the scale tabulated the weight.

Jess didn't look worried in the slightest. It must have been nice to be so confident.

Exactly thirty-eight pounds.

The crowd that had rapidly gathered let out a collective cheer surrounding Jess with congratulations.

"The event isn't over yet," Peter said, but his words fell on deaf ears. They didn't seem to care. In their minds, Jess was already the winner.

It wasn't until I saw Logan coming up the other side of the plaza that I realized Jess might have a bit of competition on his hands after all.

Logan walked next to Molly—her camera focused on the rather large catfish Molly held.

The crowd stopped cheering.

An entourage didn't surround Molly. Just Gabe, Wanda, Logan, and her cameraman.

Unlike Jess, she didn't seem even slightly disgusted by the fish she held.

"Well, looky here," Peter said with a smile. "We have another catfish." He picked up Jess's fish and tried to hand it back to Jess, but he didn't look like he wanted to touch it again. Howard was too busy directing the cameraman to get the shot that he couldn't take the fish either.

Becca pushed her way through the crowd. She looked extra bombastic with her bright blue hair curled in tight ringlets that stood out everywhere, making her look like she'd just stuck her finger in a light socket. She wore tennis shoes, tight black leggings, and a cropped fur coat.

Becca accepted the fish from Peter and held it away from her so it didn't get on her fur coat. She didn't look thrilled to have it, but she also didn't seem as grossed out by it as Jess.

How was he even a fisherman? Did people not care that he obviously hated fish? Or were his rock-hard abs and chiseled jaw-line enough for people to look past it?

"Here you go," Molly said. I turned my attention away from Jess and Becca posing with the fish back to the scale.

"I think this one might be a winner," Molly smiled, glancing over at Jess's fish with a bit of apprehension.

Howard looked downright terrified as the scale took in the fish's weight.

But his expression changed when the number came up —thirty-seven pounds, six ounces.

Molly looked around excitedly.

"Congratulations, young lady," Peter said. "You're in second place."

Her mouth dropped open. "His fish was bigger?"

"By ten ounces," Peter said.

"I demand a recount," Wanda yelled over the chatter of the crowd.

"We can do a recount," Peter said, then turned to Jess and Becca. "Can you please bring Jess's fish back over to the weigh-in station?"

He reset the scale, handing Molly her fish.

Howard and Wanda hovered over the scale, making sure everything looked perfect.

When Peter lowered Jess's fish onto the scale, the plaza was silent.

The scale seemed to take longer this time, as if it was deciding whether it should let Jess win or not. But when the number popped up the same as before—thirty-eight pounds—Jess and Howard let out sighs of relief.

"Now ours," Wanda said.

"First, let's get the length measurement of this one," Peter said, passing the fish down to me for the measurement.

"I can help," George appeared next to me, holding out his hands for the fish.

I handed him the fish, and he measured it the way Peter had instructed me to do earlier—nose to the front of the tape, pinch the tail to get every bit of length possible. We'd also learned in training that you could simply take one part of the tail or the other. You didn't have to pinch it. But Peter seemed satisfied with how George was doing it.

"Okay, let's get that other fish on the scale so we can get them back in the water." Peter held out his hands for Molly's fish.

An unwritten rule said fish this big needed to be released back into the reservoir. Not every fisherman believed in this, but I figured these two wouldn't balk at it since that's what they did on fishing shows, anyway.

"Ooh, sorry," Peter said. "Thirty-seven pounds, six ounces. But second place isn't bad." He turned to Tatiana. "Get good pictures of these ones."

Tatiana nodded and went to work, taking even more pictures than she already had.

George handed Jess's fish back to Becca and took Molly's fish to measure it.

"Get back out there and catch another one," Wanda said. "I'll make sure this one gets released."

Molly looked slightly defeated, but the day was young. She had plenty of time to catch another big one.

Becca tried to hand Jess his fish, but he brushed her off, making sure no part of the fish touched him. He was too busy signing autographs.

She replaced the fish in the cooler and turned to Howard. "Should we take it back down to release it?"

Howard looked torn. "Yeah, I'll help you." He turned to the cameraman. "Keep your lens on him and his adoring fans. If Molly comes back, make sure you get the drama."

Becca looked like she might punch Howard but kept herself back.

Each of them grabbed one of the handles on the side of the cooler and began walking awkwardly toward where Jess's boat had been pulled up on shore. It was apparent Jess wasn't worried about Molly catching a bigger fish. Otherwise, he would have hurried back out.

"Any other big ones yet?" Logan asked, turning her camera off.

"Not yet," I said. "Those two were the biggest I've seen today and in a long time."

"So you're saying it's rare to catch a catfish out of Alder Ridge Reservoir?" Logan asked in her reporter voice.

I raised my eyebrows.

"Off the record, of course," she said.

George stood up. "You don't think one of them cheated, do you?"

I shrugged. "Both of those fish were alive, moving, and will be returned to the lake." I tapped Peter on the shoulder. He'd been watching Wanda release the massive catfish. It splashed and swam away.

"What's up?" Peter said with a smile.

"Do you think it's strange that two catfish were caught so quickly in the tournament?" Logan asked.

"From what I could tell," he said slowly. "Those fish came from this reservoir today. There's no evidence of foul play."

"And you're certain about that?" George asked.

"As certain as I can be," Peter said. "If it wasn't two professional fishermen, I'd admittedly probably look into it a bit harder. But I've seen their shows. Sure, Molly is the better of the two. And I don't love that Jess's fish was bigger. But Jess has talent, too. Molly taught him well when they were together."

George did not look appeased.

"What if they come back with even bigger fish?" Logan asked.

"I'd be even less inclined to think they were cheating— provided they were different fish, of course." Peter laughed.

"You think they'd bring back the same fish, and it would be heavier?" I asked.

"It's entirely possible a fisherman could stuff a fish full of weights to make it bigger. That's part of the reason I was squeezing the fish gently to make sure that wasn't the case." He turned to Logan, who was recording again.

"Which it wasn't." He smiled. "But if they brought back a different fish—and I'd be able to tell—it wouldn't make any sense for them to bring two massive fish along with them just to cheat. It would be hard to keep them alive, and why bring two? Why not just bring one massive one?"

It made sense.

"But both of them—or rather their assistants—returned their fish to the water, right?"

We'd watched Wanda do it.

I glanced over to where Jess's boat sat partially on shore. He was climbing back inside, but Becca and Howard weren't there.

"I'm guessing so," I said. "Maybe we should have watched Howard and Becca better."

"I'm sure they did," Peter said. "I know people cheated at the last event, but this time it'll be different. And adding professionals to the mix ups the ante that much more."

I glanced at George, who still looked a bit troubled by all this. But he seemed distraught almost all the time.

Everything would be fine.

Hopefully, Molly would come in with a bigger fish so she would win, but even if she didn't, at least we knew there hadn't been cheating.

I glanced back down at Jess's boat, where he was pushing off without waiting for Becca or Howard.

He jumped up onto the bow and started the engine. It rumbled to life. It was no wonder everyone thought it was a gas engine. It definitely didn't sound like an electric one.

As he was backing away from the shore, he bent down to open a cooler . . . and an explosion engulfed the boat.

1 0

———————

Pieces of boat—and I didn't want to think about what else—flew every which way.

"Oh my God," Logan said. "Was that—"

But I was already sprinting toward the engulfed chunk of fiberglass.

Jess was on board, but maybe he was okay.

Maybe he'd gone into the water.

I covered my nose with my sleeve as I got closer, and the smoke billowed around me.

I'd been around many fires as a volunteer firefighter, but I'd never seen a boat blow up.

The water surrounding the boat was slowly taking care of the fire as the boat sunk. I waded in, looking for any indication that Jess was okay. He might have been a cheating jerk, but I didn't want another body on my hands.

A small breeze came through, blowing the smoke away and giving me the ability to see.

Pieces of blue cooler floated around my calves, but there was no sign of Jess.

"Rylie, get out of there," Ben yelled from the ranger boat in the water. "What are you doing?"

"Jess Mallard was on the boat when it blew up," I said. "Maybe he survived."

When I looked up at Ben, his eyes were wide.

"Was that an explosion?" I heard Nikki's voice come over the radio.

I clicked my mic. "Yes, by the boat ramp."

"Is everyone okay?" Nikki asked.

"No," Ben said in almost a whisper. "Everyone is not okay."

I searched the water.

My gaze found what made Ben look like he might vomit—a bloody severed hand.

I clicked my mic again. "We need the police department out here."

"What the hell happened," Howard said as I trudged out of the water.

Becca came charging down behind him. "Where's Jess?"

I sucked in a breath. Logan was filming the entire exchange. I wanted to tell her to shut the camera off, but she had a job to do.

"Let's go back up to the weigh-in station," I said.

Becca looked past me and must have seen the hand. "Oh my God," she said. "Oh my God."

Howard plowed into the water. "No," he said. "No."

Becca dropped to her knees, sobbing.

"Please, let's just go—"

"He's dead," Howard said.

I turned and found him cradling Jess's torso in his arms.

Ben gagged from the boat.

"You need to stop touching things," I said. "This could be a crime scene."

But Howard wasn't letting go. He let out a scream that you could probably hear in Wyoming.

I didn't know what to do. I'd never had to deal with a crime scene like this. How the police would find any evidence was beyond me.

I searched the water for clues that might end up getting lost.

The boat was almost completely submerged now, but it probably wouldn't sink any further since it was so close to shore.

The cooler pieces plus various fishing equipment surrounded the boat. The more I looked, the more body parts I found.

It was horrible.

Another—less guttural scream—came from behind me. I turned to find Wanda holding a practically collapsing Molly.

Becca turned and glared at her. "You did this," she said, standing and charging over to Molly. "You killed him. You just couldn't be upstaged, could you? You never knew how to let someone else have the spotlight!"

Molly looked like she might respond, but before she could, Becca's fist came into contact with Molly's nose, sending Molly toppling backward onto the ground.

"You witch," Wanda said, tackling Becca. "If anyone did this, it was you because you knew Jess was still in love with Molly."

Wanda and Becca rolled around on the ground, each landing punches. For not being a professional wrestler, Wanda held her own.

Molly sat off to the side, sobbing and begging them to stop as blood gushed from her nose.

Before I knew it, all three summies were on the scene. Tatiana was rolling around on the ground with Wanda and Becca. Whether she was joining in the action or trying to break them up was to be determined.

Sondra went to Molly's side and helped apply pressure so Molly's nose would stop bleeding.

And George was frantically looking around as if another bomb might go off at any time.

"This is some tournament you have here," Detective Bryant from the Prairie City Police Department said, coming to stand at my side.

A rush of relief came over me. Not that I'd have to deal with the scene by myself anyway, but this was his job. He knew what he was doing. Even if he looked like a regular fisherman dressed in jeans, an ugly brown fishing vest, and a circle-brimmed hat covered in flies and lures.

"It's not her tournament," Nikki said from the other side. "It's mine. And I'm pretty sure it will be the reason I'm unemployed by tomorrow." She took in the scene and then yelled out. "Everyone stop."

Her voice reverberated in my ears. Everyone paused.

Victoria stood on Nikki's other side with admiration in her eyes.

"It's not your fault someone got blown up," I said to Nikki, then turned to Bryant. "Are you on the case?"

He sighed. "I suppose I am."

The rest of Bryant's team showed up within the hour and started picking through the pieces. The fishing tournament proceeded—most people didn't know what happened. Nikki's ordered all four summies back to the weigh-in station with Peter while I spoke with Bryant.

"Before I talk to any of these . . . characters," Bryant looked around at the red-eyed, bloody-nosed, sopping-wet people standing at a distance waiting to be interviewed, "I want to hear from you."

"I'm not sure what I can tell you," I said.

"First, tell me about what you saw."

I went through all the details. Where I was standing, how Jess got on the boat, started it, opened the cooler.

Bryant nodded along as I went through everything as quickly as I could.

"Now what can you tell me about the people," he said. "About the relationships."

"They're complicated," I said. "Did you ever watch their TV shows?"

He shook his head. "I barely have time to fish myself. Why would I want to watch someone else fish?"

"I didn't either, but what I've gathered, Molly and Jess started a fishing show together while they were dating. During the show, Jess proposed, and Molly accepted. Then he cheated and broke up with her on live TV. They got divorced. Molly got the show. Jess started a new show."

I looked around at all the people.

"The woman with Molly is Wanda. I think she's her producer or something. The guy who's soaked and was in the water when you got here is Howard—Jess's producer or whatever. The guy with Molly is Gabe." I leaned in close so no one else could hear. "They're dating, but no one else knows."

Bryant looked over at them, taking mental notes.

"And the woman by Howard—"

"Is Bombastic Becca," Bryant said. "I may not watch fishing, but I know my professional wrestling."

"She is—was—Jess's girlfriend or fiancée or something. They were in a relationship."

"Right," he said, the pieces seeming to click together. "I remember when they announced her engagement. It was a big deal because she'd just gotten out of a relationship with one of the other wrestlers—Breakneck Bobby. He's a badass. Or was. After she broke up with him, he lost a bit of his edge. I actually feel bad for the guy."

The whole thing was so dramatic.

"Do you think this was murder?" I asked.

"Hard to tell," Bryant said.

"It was murder," one of the crime scene guys said. "See these?" He held up a couple of plastic crime scene bags with various pieces of what looked like electrical equipment inside. "These are the makings of a very high-tech bomb. A bomb made by a professional."

"I think it went off when he opened the cooler," I said.

The crime scene guy nodded and went back to looking through the evidence.

"So, should we start talking to people?" I asked Bryant. He quirked up an eyebrow.

"I mean, *you* start talking to people," I said. "Sorry. Old habits." Detective Bryant and I had a shaky history of him reminding me repeatedly that I'm not a police officer and needed to keep my nose out of investigation work. But recently, he'd let me help with another case.

"You can come too." He nudged me on the shoulder. "Let's start with Becca."

I followed him to where Becca was talking in hushed—yet frantic—tones with Howard.

"Is everything okay over here?" Bryant asked.

Howard whipped around and looked like he might throw a punch. "This is none of your business."

Bryant dug down into one of the pockets in his vest, pulling out a badge. "Detective Harry Bryant with the Prairie City Police Department. I'd like to speak to both of you. Separately."

"Detective? You think this was a crime?" Becca asked, her eyes big.

"We have to cover all of our bases," Bryant said.

"If anyone did it, she did," Molly said, walking up behind us, Wanda at her side. Molly was still holding a handkerchief over her nose, blood poking through. "She acts all sweet and innocent—she's not just a professional wrestler, she's an actress too—but Jess was terrified of her." She pulled the rag from her nose and showed it as evidence. "As well he should have been."

"Jess loved me," Becca said, her face turning angry again. "If you'll recall, he left you for me."

"Probably because he was scared of what you'd do to him—to his career—if he didn't." Molly's voice was nasally from pinching her nose, which made her sound like a sick little bunny rabbit.

"Afraid of me?" Becca tilted her head back and laughed. "I'm pretty sure we both know who he was really afraid of."

Bryant and I both looked at Molly.

She shrugged. "He couldn't have cared less about me."

"Okay, that's enough," Howard said. "He wasn't afraid of either of you. He was a grown-ass man who could have had any woman he wanted."

"No one leaves," Bryant said. "We need to talk to each of you. Becca, if you could follow us, please?"

I led the way up to the offices. "We can interview her in here." I opened the door, and Carmen's jaw fell open.

"Bombastic Becca?" Carmen looked like she'd just seen Elvis alive. "I didn't know you'd be here too."

"I couldn't let Jess be out there by himself, now could I?" she sniffled. "And now he's gone because of me." Her sniffle turned into a sob.

"We'll go in the back office," I said and led Becca away from Carmen, who was still in awe.

When we were all seated, Bryant started the questioning. "What did you mean back there that he's gone because of you?"

Becca wiped a tear from her face. If she was acting, she was damn good at it.

"He and I were fighting about Molly. That stupid little idiot. He still had feelings for her, but he wouldn't admit it. We were up at the bathrooms, and he stomped away back down to the boat. I couldn't stop him. If only I'd have followed him."

"You might have been blown up too," I said.

Becca let out another sob. "At least we'd be together."

"So he left the bathrooms and headed down to the boat. Then what?" Bryant asked.

"It freaking blew up, scattering pieces of my fiancé's body all over the damned lake," she yelled and slammed her fists on the table. "Did you not get the memo?"

"Okay," Bryant said, his voice soothing. "I know this is hard for you."

Her face was bright red, but she took a deep breath. "I think I'm still in shock or something."

She didn't look like she was in shock. She looked like she'd already hit the anger stage of grieving.

"Can you tell me if Jess had any enemies?" Bryant asked. "Anyone who might want him dead?"

"Uh, yeah," she said. "Molly freaking Mallard. I still can't believe he took her name. How stupid is that? Jess Mallard? Sounds ridiculous."

This lady was all over the place. I glanced over at Bryant, but he kept his focus on Becca.

"Why would Molly want to hurt Jess?"

"Because his show was hurting her show's ratings,"

Becca said. "Because she can't get anyone to care about her without Jess to support her every move. Because she's mad that he dumped her for someone prettier."

I didn't know that I would call Becca prettier. Molly had a certain girl-next-door vibe that Becca just couldn't replicate. But beauty was in the eye of the beholder. Or so they said.

"Look," Becca said, trying to contain herself. "Molly did this. Maybe all those things weren't true, but you should have seen the look on her face when she realized Jess's fish was bigger than hers. Everyone knows she's a better fisherman. But Jess keeps on beating her. Every single tournament. This was probably the last straw. Anyone in her position would have snapped."

That seemed very unlikely to me. If a skilled bomb-maker had created the bomb, they'd probably crafted it before the tournament. Which meant Molly would have had to know that Jess would beat her.

"You think she was carrying a bomb in the off chance that Jess caught a fish bigger than hers?" Bryant asked.

"Well, when you say it like that," Becca said with a sigh. "But she probably carried a bomb just waiting for a chance to kill him."

"You said you were in the bathroom when all of this took place?" Bryant asked.

"I was," she said.

"But you and Howard had the cooler up at the plaza," I said.

"What's your point?" She crossed her arms over her chest.

"Did you take the cooler back down to the boat before it exploded?" Bryant asked.

"No," she said. "I took it down to the shore and let the fish go."

"Why didn't Jess let the fish go himself?" I asked. I wanted to see if she would give the same story as Molly about Jess hating fish.

"There are certain responsibilities one has as a fiancée," she said. "Judging by the rock on your hand, you should already know that." She looked over her shoulder at the door. "My responsibility is dealing with the fish."

"Do you like fishing?" Bryant asked.

"I hate fishing," she said. "But I loved Jess, and he loved fishing."

"He did?" I asked.

She glared at me. "Of course, he did. Why else would he have a fishing show?"

We stared each other down until Bryant said, "So you dumped the fish in the water, it swam off, and then what did you do with the cooler?"

She narrowed her eyes a tiny bit more, then turned her gaze to Bryant.

"I took it to the bathroom with me," she said. "I think." She glanced down at her feet. "I don't know. I thought I did. But maybe I didn't. With the fight with Jess and everything, I can't remember."

"When Jess was finished with his photo-ops, he went to the bathrooms, right?" Bryant asked.

"Yeah," she said.

"And you fought about Molly?" Bryant asked.

"And the other women fawning all over him while I was dealing with his stupid, smelly fish," Becca said.

"And then he went down to the boat, and you stayed at the bathroom?" Bryant asked, referring to his notes.

"Yep," she said. "That's all I know. Molly did this. You should talk to her before she runs, and you can't find her." She stood.

"I have a few more questions for you," Bryant said.

"You can talk to my lawyer." Becca stood and left the room, slamming the door behind her.

I could hear Carmen say something to her, Becca shouting at Carmen, then Carmen letting out a few choice words.

Bryant looked at me. "Well, that was interesting."

"Do you think she did it?"

"I think it's entirely possible," Bryant said. "Her story doesn't seem quite right. I think we need to look for that cooler."

"And then talk to Molly?"

"Sounds like a plan."

1 2

Molly was nowhere to be found. Wanda and Gabe were also missing.

The cooler, however, was where Becca said it would be—in the women's bathroom. It wasn't surprising there were multiple coolers for a boat the size of Jess's. The one that had blown up probably held drinks or snacks or a bomb.

Peter was weighing a large trout when we walked back to the weigh-in station.

"How's it going?" I asked.

"I need to talk to you about that fish," Peter said, motioning for us to join him away from the scale where people were milling around waiting for the next fish to come in.

"What fish?" I asked.

"The one Jess caught," Peter said. "There was something wrong about that catfish."

"What do you think was wrong with it?" I asked. "I thought you said it looked just fine."

"At first, it did," Peter said. "But after George told me about his suspicions of cheating, I had him pull the picture back up, and it almost looked like the fish was a slightly different color than the one Molly had."

"Don't catfish tend to look slightly different?" Bryant asked.

"Sure," Peter said. "But this one was nearly perfect. Kind of like it was bred in captivity."

"You think Jess cheated?"

"I can't say for sure," Peter said. "Especially, now that the fish is gone, and so is Jess. But if he'd won—and not blown up—I would have suggested a polygraph test."

"A lie detector test?" I asked.

"It's in the rule book," Bryant said. "If you're suspected of cheating, you can be subjected to a lie detector test. If it were me running the event, I'd subject every winner to one whether or not they seemed suspicious."

"If Jess's fish didn't come from the reservoir, then Molly would be the winner, right?" I asked.

"As of right now, yes," Peter said. "But Molly doesn't know that. I think that's why she went back out—to catch another fish so she could rightfully beat Jess."

"And take suspicion off her," I said.

"What do you mean?" Bryant asked.

"Right now, she's one of the prime suspects in this investigation, right?"

Bryant didn't respond.

"She is because she's mad that Jess caught a bigger fish," I said. "But if she went out and caught an even bigger one, there would be no reason she'd want to kill Jess."

"Other than their horrible history," Bryant said.

"The problem is, if she doesn't catch a bigger one, how do we handle the winner?" I asked. "We can't give Jess a lie detector test now."

"And the picture won't be enough evidence to prove it wasn't a fish caught from this reservoir," Bryant said.

"I think we'll have to award Jess—or his estate, I suppose—the grand prize."

"What if we could find the fish?" I asked. "I know it's a long shot, but if that fish was bred in captivity, maybe it won't have the right survival instincts or something. Maybe it'll be easier to catch."

"It will likely die out there," Peter said. "And I suppose if it died and we could retrieve it, we could compare photos and then perhaps test to see if it came from here."

"Sounds complicated," Bryant said. "But I'm happy to know Molly didn't just vanish. That she's out there trying to catch another fish."

"I'm just throwing this out there," George said from behind us. "But what if whoever killed Jess is mad that professional fishermen were allowed into the tournament? Wouldn't Molly be in danger too?"

My heart sank. I hadn't thought of that.

I reached up for my mic. "Ranger Seven, Ranger Three?"

"Ranger Three," Ben's voice came through the speaker.

I clicked the button on my mic. "Do you have a location on Molly Mallard's boat?"

"That's affirmative," Ben said. "She's in the back of Muddy Water Cove."

My heart was racing. If I asked him to contact her, he could be in danger too. But someone needed to get her off that boat.

"Copy," I said. "Can I call you on your cell?" What I had to say would not be something that needed to be broadcast over the radio. Plus, if someone had a scanner, they might be listening. And if that someone was the killer, he'd be more likely to do something quickly if he knew his window of opportunity was closing.

"Affirm," Ben said.

"Seven clear," I said into the mic, then reached for my phone.

Ben picked up on the first ring. "What's up, kiddo?"

"I think Molly might be in danger."

"You think someone might be targeting the pros?" Ben asked.

"It's possible."

"I'll talk to her."

"Be careful," I said. "Stay far enough back that if—"

"Don't worry," Ben cut me off. "I'll be fine."

He hung up, and I turned back to Bryant, George, and Peter. "Now what?" I asked.

"Let's go back down and see if the crime scene guys have come up with anything," Bryant said.

Before I could walk away, George caught my arm. "Keep an eye out for those three fishermen," he said. "And the producers. They're all super suspicious."

I sighed. "Okay," I said, more to appease him than anything.

When we were away from the weigh-in station, Bryant muttered to himself, "All I wanted was a nice relaxing day of fishing."

"I'm sorry," I said, not sure what else to say.

"I guess it's the job," he said.

"Do you ever think about getting out of it? Retiring?"

Bryant stopped and gaped at me. "How old do you think I am?"

If I had to guess, I would have said mid-fifties, but I wasn't about to tell him that. "I don't know. Don't cops get to retire early?"

"Some cops do," Bryant said. "But I'll probably do this job until I die."

"Even if it means less time to fish?"

"The fish don't need me like the people in our city do."

I laughed.

"Any news?" Bryant asked one of the crime scene guys when we got back to the explosion site.

"It looks like the bomb was inside a blue cooler," the tech said. "And possibly inside a fish too. Or at least close to a fish."

"Is there any way to determine if there was more than one cooler in the boat?" I asked. They might have had two different coolers, and it wasn't the same cooler that Becca had taken to the bathroom then lost track of.

"There's another one," he pointed down the shoreline. "But it's red."

"I'm pretty certain the cooler they had in the plaza was blue," I said to Bryant. "But we can check the pictures."

I glanced toward the boat ramp where the three

amigos were loading their boat onto a trailer. Ray saw me and waved me over.

"I'll be right back," I said.

Bryant was so busy looking through debris, he probably didn't see me walk away.

I climbed the nearly frozen sandy beach, the slight ripples of sand almost causing me to twist my ankle in my heavy work boots. I was practically out of breath by the time I got to the boat ramp.

"What's going on over there?" Ray asked when I approached the boat Luther had just pulled out of the water with a rusty old Ford pickup.

"Looks like an explosion," Tom said.

"It was," I said. "Did you guys see anything weird out there today?"

They looked at one another and back at me. "Not that I can think of," Luther said. "Those two celebrities sure did cause a ruckus, though."

"What kind of ruckus?" I asked.

"Just hootin' and hollerin' when they caught their big fish," Tom said. "If anyone else thought they might win this competition, they were wrong by the sounds of it."

"Jess and Molly have had the two largest fish so far," I said.

"Wait." Ray looked over my shoulder and squinted. "That looks like that souped-up boat that Jess guy had."

I nodded.

Tom raised an eyebrow, Luther slapped a hand over his mouth, and Ray looked like he'd seen a ghost.

"Tell me it was just the boat," Tom said.

I shook my head no.

Luther let out a low whistle. "Poor guy."

"It's what he gets for trying to cheat," Ray said. "I believe what goes around, comes around."

"What do you mean trying to cheat?" I asked.

Luther and Tom looked at him as if they didn't want Ray to tell me whatever it was he knew.

I put my hands on my hips, resting them on my baton and pepper spray. "Now you have to tell me."

"Just go check out the guy's truck," Luther finally said. "It'll smell a bit . . . fishy. In more ways than one."

"And I think all the hootin' and hollerin' was a bit of a show," Tom said. "To make us think he just caught the fish."

The other two nodded.

"Thanks," I said and made my way to Jess's truck. It was still in the parking lot and impossible to miss with the Jess Mallard Fishing decals all over the sides.

They were right. It did smell fishy.

I peeked into the back, where it looked like there were five coolers—all different colors. If they had fish in them, big fish—prize-winning fish, we could determine Jess cheated and Molly was the rightful winner.

I reached for my phone to call Bryant, but a voice on the other side of the truck startled me. "So, did you tell them?"

I hunkered down by the tire so whoever was talking wouldn't see me.

"Tell who what?" Becca said.

"Oh, come on, you did this," the man said. "You and I both know it."

"I didn't kill Jess," she said. "I would never kill him. I love him."

"Not as much as you loved me," the voice said. "I know for a fact I was a better lover."

"How?" Becca said. "Did *you* sleep with him?"

"Molly told me."

Becca gasped. "You slept with Molly Mallard?"

"So what if I did?" the man said. "It's not like you get a say in who I sleep with anymore."

"Anymore?" Becca laughed. "Like I ever did."

"We had an open relationship," he said. "You can't get mad when you were out there sleeping with half the wrestlers."

"I most certainly was not," Becca said.

"Well, if you ask me, Jess got what was coming to him."

I heard what sounded like a slap to the face.

"You idiot," the man said. "You really need to learn to control your temper."

"Did you do it?" Becca asked.

"Do what?"

"Kill Jess," she said, stumbling over the words.

"Why would I kill him?" the man asked. "If he wants my sloppy seconds, he can have them."

Becca huffed, then stormed away down toward the crime scene.

I peeked around the tire to see what the man was doing.

He was massive—bigger than Gabe. If I had to guess, this was Breakneck Bobby. The wrestler who was completely heartbroken over Becca leaving him for Jess.

Though, he didn't seem very heartbroken.

Bobby watched her go, then pulled out a phone, dialed a number, and held it to his ear.

"She did it," he said, then hung up.

"You know," I said, standing from behind the tire. "It's not nice to accuse people of murder when you don't know whether they did it or not."

"Well, hi there," he said, flashing an incredibly charming smile. "Where'd you come from?"

"I was just coming over to check on Becca," I lied. "And then I heard you telling someone she killed Jess."

He looked down at the phone in his hand and laughed. "You might be hot, but you don't know what the hell you're talking about." He laughed again and walked away without explaining himself.

I wouldn't let him get away that easily. "Hold on," I said. "Aren't you Breakneck Bobby?"

He turned and smiled again. He probably got by on that smile his whole life. "You know my name. Now it's only fair that I know yours."

"Rylie," I said. "I'm a park ranger here. I want to know why you think Becca killed Jess."

"A park ranger, huh?" He looked me up and down. "I bet that's a cool job."

"So?" I asked.

"I have nothing to say to you about Becca." He turned again and walked away.

This time, I let him go.

When I was walking back to where Bryant was talking to Becca as she was waving her arms in the air, seemingly trying to make a point, my phone rang. The caller ID told me it was Ben calling.

"Hello?"

"Rylie, it's Ben."

"What's up?"

"Molly's not on her boat," he said. "The only person on the boat is Wanda."

"Where's Molly?"

"Wanda wouldn't say. I told her Molly might be in danger—or that she might be since she was on Molly's boat, but she didn't seem to care."

Molly was on the run. She blew up Jess and was running. Damn.

"Thanks, Ben."

We hung up, and I hurried to Bryant to let him know what I'd found. But first, I needed to tell him about Molly.

"Molly's gone," I said, not caring that Becca was still rambling on about her ex-boyfriend being a psychopath and killing Jess.

If I didn't suspect Molly so much, I might have considered Bobby as the killer.

"Hold that thought," Bryant said, holding a hand up to stop Becca from talking.

She looked like she might punch him right in the face.

"What do you mean, Molly is gone?" Bryant asked.

"Ben went to her boat, and the only one there was Wanda."

"The only one?" Bryant asked. "No cameras or anything?"

"That's what he said."

"Then she's probably somewhere filming," Bryant said.

"She probably knows she's in danger and is playing it safe."

"From what Ben said, Wanda didn't seem worried at all about Molly's safety." I shifted from one foot to the other. It was a good thing the sun had come out because it would have been frigid without it.

"Maybe that makes her a suspect," Bryant said.

"Wanda?" I asked.

"Kill the competition?" Bryant said.

"Wanda didn't do it," Becca said. "I didn't do it. My ex—Bobby—did it. Haven't you seen the news? He's so upset about us breaking up, he'd do anything to get me back."

I wanted to point out that he didn't seem that eager to get her back when I'd overheard their conversation but thought better of it.

"Can you tell me more about the coolers in the back of Jess's truck?" I asked Becca.

The look on her face told me she was caught off-guard. "I don't know what you're talking about."

"I was just up there. His truck reeks of fish. And there are at least five coolers in the back under the topper. The windows might be tinted, but I know what I saw."

"You saw wrong," Becca said. "There are no coolers. It doesn't smell like fish. And if you were over there, you heard Bobby confess to killing Jess."

Smart girl, trying to distract me from the truth. "I actually heard him accuse you." I raised my eyebrows. "Maybe you killed Jess."

She gasped, tears springing to her eyes. "I loved Jess.

We were going to start a family. I would never have killed him."

"Okay, that's enough," Bryant said, interrupting my questioning. "Why don't you go get some food and hot chocolate up at the plaza?" He motioned toward the banquet hall and looked expectantly at Becca, who wasn't moving.

"Who could eat at a time like this?" She was sobbing now. Maybe she was just acting. Who knew? But either way, she was rather annoying.

"I think we're done interviewing people for now," Bryant said. "If Molly's gone, Wanda's on the boat, the other producer—"

"Howard," Becca said.

"Howard," Bryant said. "Isn't here. And where is the ex-boyfriend?"

"I think he left in his car," I said.

"We'll just have to catch up with them another time." Bryant sighed. "But for now, I'm going to go check out Jess's truck. If he has fish in the back, that will prove he cheated."

"Meaning Molly will have won," I said.

Becca's eyes widened. "You're not seriously going to try to prove a dead man was cheating, are you?"

Bryant didn't reply to her but asked me, "Do you want to come with me to check out the truck?"

I did, but I knew the tournament was coming to a close, and Nikki would need all the help she could get. "I should probably go help with the award ceremony," I said. "If you find anything, let me know before we hand out the awards."

He nodded.

"I'll go with you," Becca said to me, her tears drying almost instantly. "I have to accept Jess's grand prize. The one he *rightfully* won."

I tried my hardest not to roll my eyes.

Becca walked a few steps behind me up to the plaza. When I glanced back at her, she stopped doing whatever she was doing on her phone and dropped it into her furry jacket pocket. "I didn't kill Jess. And Jess didn't cheat."

I would not get into an argument with her right now. If she did it, Bryant would find the evidence, and she would go to prison. And the same went for Jess cheating.

13

Peter was weighing in the last few fish as Sondra—one of the summies—stood toward the back of the line, ready to cut off additional entries the moment time ran out.

Nikki and the other rangers stood around watching. Someone may have died during her event, but Nikki seemed to be in okay spirits. Other than that, the event had gone relatively well, as far as I knew.

"Five, four, three—" the crowd began to count down as the official end of the weigh-in came to a close.

"Two—"

"Wait!" A voice said over the noise. Molly appeared at the far side of the plaza, out of breath, holding a massive fish. "I have one more."

I turned to see Becca's face turn bright red.

"Well, bring it on up," Peter said, finishing with the last fish that was in line.

Cameras, including Logan's, captured the scene from every different angle.

"This woman is a master fisherman," Logan said when she came to stand next to me, her camera still trained on Molly and the fish. "You should have seen her reel that thing in."

The fish flopped around—its massive gelatinous-looking body flexing and squirming as Peter tried to get a weight.

"This is spectacular," Peter said. "Forty-two pounds, twelve ounces. We have our winner!"

He probably wasn't supposed to say that, but he was obviously caught up in the moment.

Molly jumped up and down like a kid on Christmas Day. Becca looked like she might snap Molly's neck.

"How could she?" Becca said.

"How could she what?" Logan asked.

Becca turned as if she was just noticing Logan's existence. "She couldn't let him win even after he was blown to bits just hours ago," Becca said. "And look at her so happy. She never cared about him. She killed him. Mark my words."

Before Logan or I could say anything else, Becca turned and left.

"She's dramatic," Logan said.

"She's a pro-wrestler."

"Bombastic Becca." Logan nodded. "I'm a sports reporter, remember?"

I laughed. "Sorry." Then a thought popped into my head. "Hey, how long were you with Molly?"

"Practically all day," Logan said. "She was—is—my main story."

"Did she do anything that might implicate her in Jess's murder?"

"Not that I can think of," Logan said. "But I have her entire day recorded. We can go over it. I wouldn't mind a pizza night again, and we can work on the zip tie trick."

The last time Logan and I had a pizza night, I'd found a dead-end to an investigation I was helping with. But it was still fun.

"Pizza night it is," I said.

<hr>

Nikki awarded the grand prize to a delighted Molly. Gabe watched from a distance, beaming.

By the time I got to Garrett's, I was ready for food, beer, and bed.

"How was your day?" Garrett asked.

I was surprised he hadn't heard about the explosion.

"It was rough," I said. "A guy exploded."

Garrett looked up from the book he was reading from the other side of the couch. "I'm sorry. A guy exploded?"

"His cooler exploded, and he got caught in the blast."

"What brand of cooler? I want to make sure I don't get the same kind." Garrett smiled, then frowned when he realized I wasn't smiling. "I'm sorry, sweetie. I'm sure that wasn't very pleasant."

He held open his arms. I scooched over and let him hug me as I felt a tear roll down my cheek. I didn't usually get so upset about the cases, but this one made me sad.

"What happened?" Garrett asked, more gently this time.

I gave him a quick run-down of the day's events. "Then the next thing I knew, there was an explosion by Jess's boat."

"And Jess was on it?" Garrett asked, smoothing down my hair, careful not to touch the stitches.

"Jess was on it," I said. "And there were pieces of his body and the boat and the cooler all over the place."

"I bet that wasn't a pretty sight," Garrett said. "I'm sorry you had to deal with that."

"And to make it worse, I have no idea who did it."

"What about the police?" Garrett asked. His tone was neutral, but even though he told me not too long ago that he didn't mind me working on cases, sometimes I could tell it still bothered him.

"They're working on it," I said. "I'm sure they'll figure it out without me. I have more important things to deal with."

"Like what?" Garrett asked.

"Like our wedding," I said. "I still have to find a dress."

"One that doesn't try to kill you." Garrett laughed.

"Exactly."

"Well, besides that, everything else seems to be in order."

I sat up, wiped the tear from my face, and looked at him. "I can't wait to eat that yummy cake we tasted."

"And those flowers will be beautiful," Garrett said.

"And to get married at the Big Mountain Lodge and Resort? It's like a dream come true." I'd grown up in Big Mountain, and the lodge was one of the places I spent many weekends sledding, horseback riding, swimming, and just hanging out with friends.

He squeezed me. "I love seeing you this happy."

I stopped and thought about it. I was happy. Very happy.

But there was still that bit of panic every time I thought about actually being married. I mean, I thought of marriage as a lifelong commitment. And a lifetime was a long time.

I glanced over at Garrett, who practically had hearts in his eyes. How could I possibly be nervous about marrying such a wonderful man?

I took his face in my hands and kissed him. Gently at first. Then one thing led to another, and the next thing I knew, we were naked, rolling around in front of the fireplace. Babbitt and Fizzy traded us for the couch, where they passed out.

When we were both fully satisfied and lying on the rug, Garrett said, "I'm so happy I get to marry you."

"Me too," I said. "I'm happy I get to marry yo—"

A loud knock at the door cut off my words.

The dogs instantly woke up and started barking as if someone was trying to break into the house.

"Who is that?" I practically yelled over them.

"I don't know." Garrett yanked a blanket off the couch and pulled it over us, even though the curtains were closed and whoever was at the door wouldn't be able to see us.

The knock came again, and then a voice I thought I recognized—Molly. "Hello? Rylie, are you in there?"

I yanked on my pants and hoodie and hoped it wasn't too noticeable that I wasn't wearing a bra.

Garrett ran upstairs, both dogs tearing after him.

When I opened the door, I found a very intoxicated and weepy Molly. Makeup made little streaks down her face, and her hair looked like she'd gotten in a tussle with a cactus.

"What are you doing here?" I asked. "How did you find me?"

"Your friend, Logan, told me you'd be here." Every other word was slurred. "I need to talk to you."

"About the case?"

She looked around, fear in her eyes. "Can I just come in?"

I opened the door wider, and she walked past me. "I know I should probably tell the cops, but I thought you'd be better."

"Why?"

"Because Logan told me all about how you solve cases," she said. "She said you're brilliant."

I wouldn't have called myself brilliant, but I definitely enjoyed solving cases. "And?"

"I want you to figure out who killed Jess," she said. "Obviously, I didn't do it. Becca's been telling everyone it's me, but it's not. Logan was with me the entire day. She filmed everything."

"Maybe you planted a bomb on his boat before he got there," I said. "You were staying at the same hotel. It wouldn't have been hard for you to sneak out and put a bomb in one of his live wells or something."

She looked like she might get mad, then started laughing so hard, she nearly fell over.

"Why is that so funny?"

When she was finally finished laughing, she said, "Do you know what I had to do to get away from the cameras to meet you tonight?"

"From the look of you, you had to cross a desert and fight a bear."

She laughed again. "Is it that bad?"

"Oh," I said. "And drink the equivalent of an entire bar."

"I don't think I like your tone," she said. "But I get it. I can see why you would think it's me. Everyone thought I was still mad about Jess and Becca—even Gabe. And heck, this morning, I even threatened to kill him." She shook her head. "But I wouldn't follow through. I'm not a killer. I failed physics or whatever you need for bomb-making. I hated school. The only thing I'm good at is fishing."

"Did you sleep with Bobby?"

"Breakneck Bobby?" Her eyes widened. "No," she said. "I would never sleep with someone after they slept with Becca. She has more STDs than anyone I've ever known. I warned Jess, but he didn't believe me."

"How are you not upset at all that Jess died?" I asked. "You seemed pretty upset this morning when he said he didn't care about you."

"I am upset," she said. "But if you haven't noticed, I'm drunk too."

The implied duh in her words made me laugh a little.

"Tell me you'll help me?" Molly said. "I might go to

jail, or worse, tarnish my reputation. If I lose my show, I lose everything."

"You know you can fish without doing it on TV."

She laughed. "I wouldn't expect you to understand. Once you have money, you don't really want to give it up." She looked around at Garrett's house. "I suspect after you're married, you'll understand better. It looks like you're marrying into a wealthy situation."

I sighed. "I do just fine on my own, thank you very much."

"Sure you do," she said. "Don't you live in an apartment with reduced rent because you know the owner?"

"I—uh—how did you know that?"

"Wanda does an intensive background check on everyone I hang out with. She's super paranoid." Molly looked at her nails. "You wouldn't believe how many guys I had to break up with before she approved of Gabe."

"I thought no one knew about Gabe."

"Wanda isn't just anyone. She knows everything about my life."

"Do you think it's possible Jess didn't catch his fish at Alder Ridge?"

"Possible?" Molly laughed. "It's one hundred percent possible. He cheats at all the tournaments. How do you think he always beats me?"

"If you knew he was cheating, why didn't you tell anyone?"

"If I did, he'd out me too," she said. "I'm not proud of it, but when we were married and doing the show together, he convinced me to use some stock fish instead of actual ones we would catch. Not that the ones I caught weren't impressive—they were—they just weren't as impressive as the ones Howard brought."

"But he wouldn't touch them, so you had to rig it all up?"

"Exactly," she said. "Which makes me just as bad as him."

"But you're doing things the right way now, right?"

"Logan has it all on camera," she said. "Even though Jess was dead, I still felt some stupid sense of accomplishment for beating his cheating with the real deal. That's probably why I was celebrating so much at the award ceremony. And after. And later. And why I'm so drunk now." She let out a small laugh.

"How did you get here?" I peeked through the curtain to find an empty street and driveway. I parked Cherry Anne in the garage next to Garrett's car.

"My driver dropped me off," she said. "I told him to stay close in case you wouldn't let me in."

"Okay," I said, trying to get back to the conversation at hand. "So you want me to look into this case and clear your name?"

"Yep," she said. "And I want you to do it immediately. I have another event in a week. The promos start in two days. I absolutely will not show my face unless you can tell the public who did this."

My dad used to tell me, *"Everyone else's emergencies are not necessarily your own. You don't have to tend to their emergencies unless you want to."* This seemed like the perfect time to put that into practice.

"I'm sorry," I said. "But I don't think I'll be able to

solve a case in two days. If you're looking for some sort of guarantee, I can't give it to you."

"I'll give you a million dollars," she said. "Cash."

I nearly passed out. She was drunk. She didn't know what she was saying.

"I thought you said a ten-thousand-dollar prize was a lot," I said. "Now, you're offering me a million dollars?"

"I said every little bit helps," she said. "The money I earn from the tournaments is my blow money."

"As in drugs?" I didn't want to hear this. I didn't need her to tell me all the crazy things that happened in the film industry.

"Not drugs," she said. "Like, I can blow it on whatever I want. But the million dollars will come from my investments. I may be drunk, but I think investing a million dollars in clearing my name will be worth it." She pulled out her phone and sent a text. "There. Now it's in writing."

My phone dinged from the end table next to the couch.

"So?" She raised her eyebrows expectantly.

"And what if I can't?"

She turned toward the door.

"Then you won't get a million dollars." She shrugged. "But we can still be friends."

I almost laughed. This had to be a joke.

"Think about it, but think fast." She opened the door. "Your time starts now."

"She offered you a million dollars to solve the case?" Shayla asked the next morning at our apartment. I had to go back to get some clean clothes and tell Shayla everything. "And you agreed?"

"I didn't agree," I said, taking a bite of my cereal. "But I didn't not agree either."

Shayla sighed. "You know this won't be easy, right?"

"I know," I said. "There are about a hundred different possible suspects. Trust me. I wrote it all out last night."

"Like who?"

"Well, Molly herself," I said. "Though I doubt she'd hire me to figure out who the killer was if she was the killer."

"It happens," Shayla said. "But Molly seems to be of sound mind and not one to test her killer abilities."

If only Shayla would have seen Molly drunk off her ass the night before.

"So not Molly," I said. "But Becca, Wanda, Gabe, Bobby, Howa—" I hesitated. "Where was Howard?"

"When?" Shayla asked.

"I saw him with Becca after the explosion, but then he and their cameras disappeared." I thought about this for a minute. "They didn't take Jess's truck. It was still in the parking lot."

I pulled out my phone and started on a text message to Bryant.

Did you find anything in the truck?

I hit send.

"Well, if Jess was dead," Shayla said when I looked up from my phone, "they wouldn't have needed to keep filming, would they?"

"No," I said. "But Howard seemed pretty broken up about Jess's death. I'm just surprised he left."

"Maybe you should talk to him," Shayla said. "With Bryant, of course."

Speaking of Bryant, his text came back through.

Truck was gone.

"The truck was gone?" I said aloud.

"What truck?" Shayla asked.

"Jess's truck," I said. "It smelled fishy, and there were several coolers in the back. I'm pretty sure he was storing fish in there so he'd win."

"He cheated?"

I nodded. "Molly told me so."

I texted Bryant back.

We need to talk to Howard. Today.

"I texted Bryant to see if he'll meet me."

"Be careful," she said. "I know I tell you that all the time, but I don't want you to get hurt."

My phone dinged.

You read my mind.

I put my bowl in the dishwasher and hugged Shayla. "You're the best friend a girl could ask for."

Bryant met me at the ritzy hotel where Molly and Jess were staying.

"I hear you got an offer you couldn't refuse," Bryant said. "If you keep going down this path, you'll need to get your private investigator license."

I'd never wanted to be a cop, but a PI? That might not be so bad.

My mind darted to Garrett. He'd never be on board for me being a PI.

It didn't matter. I enjoyed being a park ranger. And eventually, I'd move onto something else. I just didn't know what that was yet.

When Bryant knocked on Howard's hotel room door, there was shuffling and a couple of squeals before Howard opened the door wearing nothing but a pair of briefs.

"Please put some clothes on," Bryant said.

Howard was almost as hairy as a bear and about as big around. He left the door open when he walked deeper into the room to retrieve his pants.

Bryant took this as an open invitation to enter.

The room was large, but not as large as you'd expect from such a fancy place.

"Is there someone else here?" Bryant asked.

Howard buttoned his pants and slipped a t-shirt over his head. "No."

"Are you sure?" Bryant's gaze flickered to the curtains that almost reached the floor.

Almost.

If they had, they would have covered up the two feet with bright pink toenails.

"Fine," Howard said. "I'm not alone."

"Whoever is behind the curtains, please come out," Bryant said.

Becca stepped from behind the curtains. She was completely naked.

Bryant hesitated before averting his eyes.

Becca looked pleased with herself. Which, if I looked like her naked, I would be too.

I glanced down at my thighs. I needed to solve this case, but even a million dollars wouldn't make me thinner.

I vowed to go on a run right after we were done talking to Howard.

"Put some clothes on," Howard barked.

She slowly put her clothes on as Bryant focused on an invisible speck on the wall furthest from her.

"There," she said. "Better?" She put on short shorts and a see-through tank-top without a bra. It wasn't a huge change, but at least she was clothed.

"We're here to talk to you about Jess's death," I said, ignoring her blatant attempt at attention.

"I already told you—" Becca started, but Howard cut her off.

"They're here to talk to me," he said. "This is my room. They knocked here. Don't be an idiot. And stop acting like that. You were just caught sleeping with the producer of your dead fiancé's show. By the police. Can't you see how this looks?"

"Like I'm trying to sleep my way into getting my own show?" she asked. "Because if that's the case, that's exactly what it should look like."

Howard sighed, then turned his attention back to us. "What can I do for you?"

"Where did you go after Jess died?" I asked.

Bryant didn't seem to mind that I'd taken the lead on asking the questions.

"The camera crew and I packed up. I had to talk to the big-wigs about what we would do with the footage."

"What footage?" I asked.

"The footage of Jess blowing up," Howard said.

Becca turned an ugly shade of green and ran to the bathroom. We could hear her vomiting through the door.

"You have that on film?" Bryant asked.

Howard nodded. "It's not pretty, but it's part of Jess's story."

"You can't seriously be considering airing that footage?" I asked.

"I'm not," Howard said. "The network would never go for it. Family TV and all."

"Would you be willing to turn that footage over to the police?" Bryant asked. "It could help us figure out who killed Jess."

"You think this was murder?" Howard asked.

"It's not likely that it's anything else," I said. "The crime scene crew found parts of a bomb."

"That could have been anything—part of the motor," Howard said. "It was modified, you know? There were lots of wires and stuff that wouldn't normally be on a fishing boat."

"They're looking into it more closely," Bryant assured him. "But about that footage?"

"I'll see what I can do," Howard said. "The network is pretty persnickety about who they hand out footage to."

"I can get a warrant," Bryant said.

"Well, that would definitely speed them up," Howard laughed.

"What about his truck," I said. "What happened to Jess's truck and boat?"

"It's in the parking lot," Howard said. "But you'll need a warrant for that, too. Sorry." His apologetic voice didn't sound so apologetic.

"Do you have any idea who might have wanted Jess

dead?" I asked, then added quickly, "If this was, in fact, a murder?"

"It was probably Gabe," Howard said. "You know, the big guy—Molly's boyfriend?"

"I don't think they're dating," I said, trying to protect Molly's privacy.

"Then you're blind," Howard said. "Maybe after working behind a camera all these years made me more perceptive, but they're definitely in love. Not just boinking."

Bryant sucked in a breath and let it out slowly. I could sense his frustration rising.

"Why would Gabe want Jess dead?" I asked.

"Because Molly wasn't over Jess," Becca said, coming out of the bathroom. "She called him all the time."

"Molly called Jess?" I asked.

Becca nodded. "It was so pathetic. She'd say she missed him, and he'd hang up on her. I almost felt bad for her." She wiped her mouth with the back of her hand. "Just kidding, I didn't feel bad at all."

I couldn't believe how horrible she was.

"If it wasn't Gabe," I said. "Who else might it have been?"

"Bobby," Becca said. "I don't know how many times I have to tell you. It was Bobby."

"Bobby was at the lake yesterday?" Howard asked. "And I didn't get it on film?"

Becca shrugged.

"If you want your own show, make sure the camera gets the good parts," Howard said. "You can't go sneaking around creating drama with no one to see."

"Does that mean you're giving me a show?" Becca asked.

"I'll run it by the network," Howard said. "But you have to at least act like you're sad Jess died."

She instantly turned on the waterworks and gave an impressive show of hysterics. Just as quickly as she'd turned them on, she turned them off. "How's that?"

Howard sighed, then turned to us. "Any other questions you might have?"

"No questions," Bryant said. "But I'll be getting those warrants. Don't leave town."

15

I laced up my running shoes and clipped Fizzy's leash to his collar. We'd been running almost every morning, and it felt good. Though the pounds weren't melting off like I hoped they would have.

Garrett's neighborhood was breathtakingly beautiful, and the people were so friendly. Everyone I passed waved at Fizzy and me.

It would be a nice place to live, but it would be hard leaving Shayla.

She probably wouldn't mind since she and Seamus would have more room without me. He stayed over almost every night now.

When I turned a corner, I heard children playing on a playground. Our kids would go to this elementary school.

Our kids.

Mine and Garrett's.

I didn't know whether it was panic or excitement welling in my chest. I had always wanted kids, but I still felt young. Too young. But I wasn't too young. Many of my friends from high school had already had kids and were living their lives as mothers.

Why was it so hard for me to consider being a mom?

I ran past a cute little girl with blonde ringlets who waved with her chubby little hand. I waved back and smiled.

It was excitement.

I wanted to be a mom.

And Garrett would be a great dad.

I turned a corner and almost ran straight into a giant of a man.

Breakneck Bobby.

He smiled. "I hoped I'd find you out here."

My insides clenched. I didn't have it in me to fight someone off. I might have gone a little too hard with the run out the gate.

Fizzy snarled, probably sensing my distress.

"Whoa there, buddy," Bobby said. "I'm not gonna hurt your mama."

"If you're not here to hurt me, why are you stalking me?"

"I need to talk to you about the case," Bobby said.

"Oh, now you want to talk to me?"

"I had a change of heart," he said. "Becca did it."

"Why would she kill Jess?"

"So she could have her own show," he said, taking a step toward me.

Fizzy snapped, and he stepped back. Fizzy was an incredibly gentle dog most of the time, but sometimes his protective side came out a bit strong. Especially when he felt the need to defend me.

"She's probably sleeping with the producer as we speak," he said.

I didn't have the heart to tell him she already had.

"Some would say you have motive to kill Jess," I said.

"Who? Becca?"

I shrugged.

"Of course, she'd say that. She wants to do everything she can to rip out my heart." Tears welled up in his eyes. "I thought it was bad enough that she dumped me, but trying to frame me for murder—to put me in jail—is so much worse."

"It does make sense," I said. "Especially if you were jealous of their relationship."

"Oh, I was jealous, all right." He huffed. "But I have a lot of emotions, and none of them made me kill anyone."

I didn't know what to believe. He seemed to be telling the truth, but maybe he was a good actor too. I mean, he was a professional wrestler like Becca.

"Just go over there, check out her room."

"Why her room?"

"Don't you know why her name is Bombastic Becca?"

I shook my head. "It's catchy?"

"And because she made bombs for the military."

"You're just now telling me this?" I tipped my head back and closed my eyes.

He shrugged. "Do you need a lift to the hotel?"

He may have shown his gentler side with the tears and such, but there was no way I was getting in a car with him. "No, thanks."

"But you are going to the hotel, right?"

"Yes," I said.

"Good," he said. "Because I think they're checking out tomorrow."

"Good to know," I said. "Anything else?"

"If you're free sometime, we could get drinks."

I turned and ran the other way.

I called Bryant on my way to the hotel to let him in on what Bobby said. He told me he'd meet me at the hotel after he finished a report. Apparently, he didn't think it was terribly urgent to search Becca's hotel room.

I waited in the parking lot for about a half-hour before deciding I'd just go up and talk to Becca myself. She might have been a bit of a nut job, but she didn't seem too dangerous. Unless she was building a bomb and decided to blow me up or something.

The hallway leading to her room was long. I vividly remembered watching Molly yelling at Jess down this same hallway. When I got to the room, the door was already slightly ajar.

When I pushed it open, the scene in front of me almost made me gag.

Blood was everywhere.

Then I heard something in the bathroom.

Someone.

"Oh God," the voice said. "No. Please, no."

I tip-toed inside, careful not to step in any of the blood.

"Where's my phone? I need to call the police," the voice, now recognizable as Molly's, said.

I pushed open the door to find Molly holding a blood-soaked towel over Becca's chest. Becca's eyes were open, but there was no one there.

She was dead.

"What's going on in here?" I asked.

Molly turned but didn't remove her hands from the towel.

"She's bleeding. We need an ambulance. Call an ambulance, Rylie."

I pulled out my phone and dialed nine, then one, but a hand was on my back before I could finish.

I whipped around, ready to clock someone on the side of the head, only to find Bryant.

"I'll call it in," he said.

I nodded, and he spoke into his mic, talking to dispatch, requesting an ambulance.

Other than the blood, there was so much more in the room.

Junk.

Bomb-making junk.

Wires and switches and blocks of what I guessed were the explosives.

Exactly what I expected to find—what Bobby told me I'd find.

"Is someone coming?" Molly asked from the bathroom.

I peeked inside again, careful to keep my gaze on Molly and not the rest of the scene. "The police are here, and the ambulance is on its way."

"She'll be okay, right?" Molly asked frantically. "She will. She has to."

"What happened?" I asked.

"I don't know," Molly said. "I got a phone call from the front desk requesting that I come to Becca's room. The door was cracked open when I got here. I knocked, but no one answered, so I let myself in. That's when I saw the blood. All the blood. And the bomb stuff. Holy crap. How did this happen? Who did this? Why?"

"It's okay," I said. She did the same thing as I did when I got flustered—verbal vomit. Though my ex had coined that phrase, and I hated it at the time, I'd embraced my vomitous words when I got nervous and take the phrase as my own. "It will be okay."

Bryant tapped me on the shoulder and motioned for me to step out of the way. "Molly Mallard, you're under arrest."

Molly gasped.

I gasped.

"What? Why?" Molly looked torn as to whether she should stay and keep pressure on a dead woman's chest or stand and allow herself to be arrested. "I didn't do anything wrong."

"Please stand up so the paramedics can take over," Bryant said.

She stood, and another officer handcuffed her while the paramedics rushed into the bathroom.

I moved toward the door, trying to get out of the way.

"Why are you arresting me?" Molly demanded.

"Murder," Bryant finally said. "Of Jess Mallard and Becca Bullsworth."

"Murder?" Molly and I both said at the same time.

The officer who had arrested Molly took her out of the

room. As she was leaving, she yelled, "Two million, Rylie. By tonight. Two million."

"You can't be serious arresting Molly," I said to Bryant. "Do you see all of this bomb-making equipment? It's obvious Molly didn't do it. Becca did."

"Molly planted it here," Bryant said. "There's more hidden in her room."

"There are bomb-making materials hidden in Molly's room?"

"More than what is lying around here," Bryant said. "I suspect Molly was trying to frame Becca and Becca surprised Molly." He paused. "We thought we had a tight enough perimeter to grab Becca before she went to her room, but we also didn't think Molly would stab her to death."

"That's quite the assumption on only being at the scene for less than ten minutes."

"I've been here longer than you," he said. "I was already at the hotel when you called me. I didn't think you'd come in without me, though."

"But—"

"It's okay," he said. "We're not always right every time."

That may have been true, but this time I knew I wasn't wrong. At least about Molly not killing Becca. Becca was the actress, not Molly.

"What about the cameras that follow Molly around? Wouldn't they be able to attest to her whereabouts?"

"She was supposed to be with Wanda at the reservoir fishing again today, but when we called out to the reservoir, one of the rangers told us they were shooting b-roll and didn't need Molly for those shots."

"It wasn't Molly," I said. "Check the front desk. They called her phone and told her to come here. To Becca's room. Someone is setting her up. Becca was the bomb-maker, not Molly."

"What do you mean Becca was a bomb-maker?"

"She made bombs in the military. That's why they called her Bombastic Becca."

"Who told you that?" he asked.

"Bobby," I said. "He tracked me down on my run."

"And told you Becca was responsible for Jess's death?"

"And that she makes bombs professionally." A thought dawned on me. "Maybe Bobby did it and is trying to set up Molly. That's why he wanted me to come over here so quickly so I could catch Molly in the act. And then while she was in here, he was planting bomb-making supplies in her room."

"I don't know that I buy it," Bryant said. "But I'll check into it if you want me to."

"It wasn't Molly," I said. "I'm certain."

"I know she was your friend, but sometimes we have to see things as they are rather than how we'd like them to be."

I'd dated enough jerks to know how important it was to see things as they were. I'd spent plenty of time seeing things how I wanted them to be. That's why I knew I wasn't seeing this thing wrong. Molly didn't do it. And I didn't need a two-million-dollar incentive to want to clear her name.

16

As I was leaving the hotel, I heard someone shouting. The police were still in the room working on evidence, and the hallway was completely clear.

The shouting sounded like it was coming from Howard's room, and when I got closer, it was Howard's voice echoing from his wide-open door.

"What the hell will I do now?" His voice was panicked. I flattened myself against the wall to listen without him seeing me. "I need a show, and my actors keep dying." He paused, then said. "I know, but still. She might not have been the best choice of leads, but people liked to see her in all her crazy glory."

I wanted to walk in and tell him to be a bit more respectful of the dead but thought better of it.

"No way," he said. "There is no way in hell I'm teaming up with her. She can suck it for all I care." He paused. "I know we both need shows now, but she is my enemy. You should know better than to—" he stopped talking. And then something crashed against a wall.

Before I could move, he barged through the doorway, turned down the hallway, and nearly plowed into me.

"Were you listening to my phone call?" His eyes were angry. He looked more like a bear now than he had with his shirt off.

"No," I lied. "I was just walking by. I went to talk to Becca but—"

"I know," he said. "It's terrible. Tragic. And now I have nothing. But neither does Wanda. Her girl is going to prison for a long time. And good riddance. How dare she kill two of my biggest stars?"

"I don't think she—"

"She did," he said. "Everyone is talking about it."

"How?" I asked. "It only just happened."

Howard shrugged. "News travels fast in show business."

"Did you see anyone going up or down this hall? Maybe Bobby?"

He shook his head. "Bobby? Why would he be here?"

"That's what I'm trying to figure out," I said, trying to come up with something. "Maybe he came to win Becca back."

"Becca never loved him. Becca never loved anyone other than Becca. She would have done anything to get what she wanted. And she almost got it. Until she got herself murdered. It was probably that stupid mouth of hers. She always had a way of saying the wrong thing at the wrong time." He looked me up and down. "You're a park ranger, right?"

I hesitated. Why did that matter? "Uh, yeah."

"Have you ever thought about doing any television work?"

I almost laughed out loud. I'd once been a viral YouTube star. And not for the best of reasons. "No. I'm not what you'd call television material."

"You should consider it." He pulled a business card from the pocket of his slacks. "Here's my card. I'll be in touch."

He walked past me, closing his hotel room door securely behind him. "Now, if you'll excuse me. I have to go get a new phone."

I rushed to the reservoir to find Wanda, Gabe, and the camera crew packing up in a hurry.

"You heard?" I asked.

"They took her to jail?" Wanda asked. "Why? She didn't kill anyone."

"I know," I said. "But the evidence is pretty damning."

"I did it," Gabe said. "I killed them."

"Shut up, Gabe," Wanda said. "You were here with me the entire day. Giving the police a false confession won't help Molly. It'll only keep them from finding the actual murderer."

Gabe looked like a puppy who had been told to get off the couch.

"Do you think there's any way Molly would have done this?" I asked.

Wanda thought about it for a minute. "She didn't like

either of them," Wanda said. "But I don't think she has it in her. Me, on the other hand . . ."

"You what?"

"No," she said. "I didn't do it. But sometimes I wish I had. Especially now. Molly doesn't deserve to be in prison for something she didn't do. She's the sweetest girl I've ever met."

Wanda's phone rang.

"Hold on. I need to get this." She picked it up. "What do you want?"

She paused, and I could hear a man's voice on the other end.

"They want us to what?" She waited. "Yeah, that's not going to happen. I'd rather eat dirt than work on a project with you."

I assumed it was Howard. He'd gotten a new phone awfully quickly.

My phone buzzed with a text message from Logan.

Pizza, zip ties, and video footage tonight?

I typed back.

Perfect timing. My place or yours?

Mine. You can bring the pizza.

. . .

Deal.

"Did Howard ask you to be on television?" Wanda asked as she dropped her phone into her purse.

"He did, but I—"

"Listen to me." She held up a hand. "You absolutely cannot work with him. He will destroy your life. If you want to work with anyone, you'll want to do it with me." She, too, gave me a business card. "Think about it. Anything he offers, I can double."

"I—but—"

"We have to go," Wanda said. "I'll do everything I can to bail Molly out of jail tonight."

"And I'll do everything I can to clear her name."

"How much did she offer you?" Wanda asked.

I was surprised Wanda knew Molly had offered me money.

"Two million by tonight," I said.

"Make it three if you have it figured out by tomorrow."

Three million dollars. These people were handing out hypothetical money like it was rocks. But at least she'd given me an extra day.

"I'll see what I can do."

17

Every time I pulled into Logan and Eli's driveway, I was overcome with awe. Then a bit of jealousy. Eli had apparently liked me at one point. It was hard not to think about what life might be like if I'd called the number he'd scrawled on my jersey. Though I was certain if I really wanted a house like theirs—a verifiable mansion—Garrett would have done everything within his powers to make it happen.

The valet parked Cherry Anne, and Logan opened the front door, leading me through the foyer with the huge chandelier and into the kitchen. She poured each of us a Bud Light with fresh lime from the beer tap installed on the countertop, then led me downstairs to the theater room.

"Before we watch the video, I want to try the zip tie thing."

I'd hoped she would have forgotten. But when she pulled out several bags of zip ties, I knew I wasn't getting out of it.

"Let's start with the little ones," I said.

We each zip-tied each other's hands in front of us to start.

"Now what?" Logan asked.

I tried to remember what George had taught me. "Raise your arms above your head and then bring them down over your stomach or hip as fast as you can while pulling your hands apart."

She laughed nervously. "We won't ever have to use this, but it's still fun to practice. We can never be too prepared, right?"

I nodded.

"I'll go first."

She sucked in a breath and raised her arms. Just as she was about to pull them down, I yelled, "Wait."

She stopped with her arms in front of her.

"Tighten the zip tie first," I said, remembering what George had told me.

"Tighten it?" She gave me the exact look I imagined I'd given George.

"He said it'd hurt less and work better." I shrugged.

"Okay." She sounded skeptical but tightened the tie with her teeth. "That good?"

"I suppose so," I said.

She lifted her arms again and took another breath. Then—without warning—she yanked her arms down across her flat stomach, and the zip tie popped right off.

"That didn't even hurt," Logan said. "You try."

I tightened my zip tie and made the same motion. Mine popped off too, but it did hurt.

"Let's try a bigger one," Logan said. "I would think a

kidnapper would use something more substantial than those little wimpy zip ties."

She was right, but I didn't want to. My wrists already hurt from the wimpy ones.

But she was holding the tie out, waiting for me to zip her up.

"Ooh, and let's do it behind our backs," she said.

I laughed. She was crazy.

We must have looked like psychotic worms as we tried to shimmy our arms down around our butts and then pull them around our legs.

We were laughing so hard by the time we got them to the front that I wasn't sure we'd have the energy to free ourselves from the zip ties.

I was wrong.

Logan lifted her arms in the air and pulled them down like an expert, the tie popping right off.

She was tiny. Probably not more than a hundred pounds. If she could do it, so could I.

I lifted my arms and pulled down. Pain shot through my wrists, causing me to yelp.

The zip tie didn't come off.

Blood seeped out from beneath the tie.

"I think we should cut it off," I said.

But Logan stood with her hands on her hips. "A little blood and pain shouldn't keep you from getting yourself free. Do it again."

I wanted to tell her to shove it. She sounded like George. But I also didn't want to ruin our relationship . . . or seem like a wimp.

My wrists practically cried out, begging me not to do it

again. But I did. And this time, when I pulled my arms down, the zip tie popped off easily.

"See? That wasn't so bad," Logan said. "Okay, let's watch the video and eat pizza now."

And just like that, we moved on from the zip ties.

"Where should I start?" Logan asked when we were comfy on the oversized leather couches with pizza in one hand and beer in the other.

"How about the beginning of the event," I said, my mouth half-full of pizza. "Whenever you started recording."

She fast-forwarded through the recordings taken before the event when Molly was in a bikini and went straight to where Molly was handing out donuts.

"Ooh, this is a good part," Logan said.

Just then, Jess's truck pulled up in the line, and Molly tried to hand a couple of donuts to whoever was in the passenger seat. I couldn't tell from the angle whether it was a man or a woman, but whoever took the donuts threw them back, hitting Molly square in the face.

"Oh my goodness," I said. "Who threw those? Was it Becca?"

"Becca didn't show up until later." Logan fast-forwarded the footage to where Becca pulled up in a little car about a half-hour after Jess.

Molly handed her a donut with a smile, and Becca accepted it. They even chatted for a couple of minutes before the next car came up behind her.

"That seemed oddly cordial," I said. "I thought they hated each other."

"From what I could tell throughout the day, they didn't seem to have much animosity toward each other, but lots toward Jess. Until he died, of course. Then everything bubbled to the surface."

"Makes sense," I said. "Not to speak ill of the dead, but Jess didn't seem like the best significant other."

"He flirted with so many women, it made me want to vomit," Logan said. "Aren't we lucky we have such wonderful men in our lives?"

"Definitely."

"So the day was pretty boring. Ooh, except this part." She fast-forwarded to what seemed like mid-morning. "Sorry, I'll back it up after I show you this."

When she stopped the recording, she burst out laughing. "Watch this."

I couldn't help but laugh along with her, unsure what to expect.

"This was after the explosion, when we walked back down to the shore," Logan said. "Keep watching."

The screen showed Molly casting and reeling, the audio was silent. Until I heard a gasp.

"Oh my goodness," Molly said, her reeling motion coming to a halt. "Do you see that?"

The camera whipped toward the concrete path that surrounded the reservoir. And when it stopped, it was focused on one of our regulars.

Naked guy.

We watched as he bounded down the path, waving to all the fishermen as he did.

Logan was gasping for air, she was laughing so hard. "I couldn't." Gasp. "Believe it." Gasp.

"That's naked guy," I said, laughing along with her. "He's at the reservoir all the time."

"He just kept running," she said, pausing the video and then backing it up. "Molly and I were stunned. Then we couldn't stop laughing."

"Did one of the rangers talk to him?" I asked.

"I think Nikki did," she said. "But I only saw her drive by a few minutes later shaking her head."

"We've learned to live with him." I shrugged. "Okay, back to the day."

"Right, back to the day." Logan cleared her throat. "I thought Molly would head out on her boat, but she decided to give the shore a try first. Within three casts she caught her first catfish."

Logan expertly captured Molly carrying the huge fish up the beach and to the weigh-in station.

"Wait," I said. "Back up a minute."

She paused and went back.

"Do you see that person in the background?" I moved closer to the screen. "It looks like they might be going to Jess's boat."

She paused and zoomed in.

"And they're carrying a cooler," I said. "A blue one."

"Is that important?"

"They think the bomb was inside a blue cooler."

"Then that might be the killer," Logan said. "But I can't make them out. They look like they are wearing all black with white shoes of some sort."

"Maybe we can pick them out somewhere else," I said. "Keep going."

We went through the rest of the day. Molly laughed when she nearly fell into the lake after pulling in a large—but not large enough—wiper. She cried when she talked about how Jess always beat her at the tournaments. She subtly got close to mentioning his cheating but stopped short of any true accusation. Logan asked a bunch of questions, and they chatted a lot, but we never saw anyone with the same outfit on again.

The last shot was of Molly claiming her prize at the award ceremony. She looked thrilled. Way too happy after her ex-husband had just died. It was too bad she wasn't an actress like Becca had been.

"Does any of that help?" Logan asked, turning off the video and turning on the lights.

"I didn't see anyone that matched the person with the cooler."

"How did you feel about Molly?" Logan asked. "I mean, I know she was arrested for killing two people."

"I don't think she did it." I thought for a minute. "Maybe it's my emotions taking over because she seemed so friendly, but even though she didn't show much sadness about Jess's death, I don't think she had it in her to kill him. I really believe she was just excited to have finally proven herself. Fair and square."

"From what I sensed, there was a lot of animosity that went past the cheating," Logan said.

"Yeah, there was a bunch of crap that Molly had to deal with. NDAs and the like."

"About what?"

I shook my head. "Sorry," I said. "Not my story to tell."

Logan nodded. "I respect that." She pulled one of her legs up and hugged her knee. "So now what?"

"Now we need to figure out if anyone has seen the person in that video—the one with the white shoes and the cooler."

"I'll send a clip of the video for you to reference."

"Thanks," I said. "I'll see what I can do."

"And I think we should try the industrial-sized zip ties." Logan bounced up from her seat. "Just one time."

The next day I showed up for my shift early with throbbing wrists. Logan's idea of one time was not one time at all. If that wasn't bad enough, I hadn't been able to sleep once I got home. My mind raced between the possibilities of who could have planted that bomb.

I thought if I got to the reservoir before the gates opened, I could do a lap around the crime scene and see if I remembered anything.

But when I got there, the police were still combing the area.

"Hey there," Bryant said. "What are you doing here so early?"

I yawned. "I'm opening the reservoir." I took a sip of my nonfat coffee and sighed. The scale still hadn't moved. I was so close to throwing in the towel and going back to my candy bar in a cup version of coffee.

"From what I understand," Bryant said. "The reservoir doesn't open for another half hour."

"Okay, so I wanted to come out and see if anything tripped a memory for me."

"And?"

"Nothing," I said. "It was a bit of a blur. But I did talk to Logan—the sports reporter who was assigned to Molly."

He nodded.

"She and I watched the footage she got. It looked like someone dressed in all black with white shoes had a blue cooler heading toward Jess's boat before it blew up."

Bryant's eyes lit up. "Is it time-stamped?"

"Yep," I said, pulling out my phone. I took off my glove so I could use my fingertips on the touch screen. I really needed to invest in some fancy gloves that worked with a phone. Heck, if I solved this case by the end of the day, I'd have three million dollars. I could probably buy the entire touch screen glove company.

I started the video. "And if you'll notice, it can't be Molly because she's carrying a fish to be weighed in."

Bryant ran a gloved hand over his stubbly chin. "Provided that was the cooler containing the bomb, then Molly wouldn't have been the one who planted it." He sighed. "Though she could have been the one who put it in the cooler. Maybe she was working with someone."

"If she was, she seemed pretty surprised to find Jess dead."

"Everyone did." He shook his head. "These people are actors. Be careful who you trust."

I turned off my phone and returned it to the pocket of my coat. "I'll be careful."

"Speaking of acting, I hear they offered you the opportunity to be on television."

I laughed. "Jealous?"

"Not a chance," he said. "I couldn't possibly be on TV. I'm too—"

"Cranky?" I laughed. "Mean?"

He looked at me with a glare.

I raised my eyebrows. "You're only proving my point."

His composure cracked, and he actually sort of smiled. "Are you going to do it?"

"No," I said. "I have zero television ambition."

"I hate to admit this, but you'd be good. People like you."

"They might like me in real life, but when a camera is pointed at me, I would likely turn into a mumbling mess."

He shrugged, and we stood in silence for a moment.

"Have they found anything else?" I asked.

"Nothing significant," Bryant said. "But we have to look. Mix sand, water, and an explosion, and you have quite a messy crime scene."

"I'm sure." I glanced at my watch. "I should probably go open the gates."

"Keep people away from the scene if you can," Bryant said. "The caution tape can only do so much."

"I'll see what I can do."

When I got to the gate, there were probably fifty cars lined up. On a normal day, there might have been three. The news had done a pretty good job of keeping the location of Jess's death secret. Until last night.

I opened the gate and stood to the side, watching car after car zoom past.

"What are all these people doing here?" Ray said, pulling up to a stop next to me as cars passed by. All three amigos were in the old Ford pickup with their shiny new boat on a trailer behind them.

"I think it has to do with the news report about Jess dying here," I said.

"I bet they're here to pay their respects," Ray said. "Did you ever look in the back of that guy's truck?"

I'd meant to ask Bryant about that. "They wouldn't let us. Said we needed a warrant." I leaned in. "But when I peeked, there were definitely fishy-smelling coolers."

"I knew it," Tom said from the middle seat. "I bet he cheated at all the tournaments. That pretty boy didn't know a thing about fishing."

Ray and Luther looked at him as if he'd grown another head.

"Why didn't you guys report the truck the day of the tournament?" I asked. "I mean, other than nudging me in that direction."

"We did," Luther said. "But with the explosion and all, it kind of went by the wayside."

"Were you around when the boat blew up?" I asked.

"Nah," Luther said. "And it's a good thing. I think we all might have jumped out of the boat to take cover. Nam and all."

The three of them had fought in the Vietnam War. "I know I tell you this all the time," I said. "But—"

"Thank you for your service," they all said in unison.

"I want you to know I appreciate you."

"Now stop that," Luther said. "You're gonna make us fog up the truck."

"Can we go fishing now?" Ray said, obviously not thrilled about all the emotion coming from his friends.

"Sure thing," I said. "Thanks for your help."

I needed to talk to Bryant about the back of Jess's truck and see if he'd gotten a warrant. Whether the cheating had anything to do with the murder was still up for debate, but sometimes clues came from places you would never have expected.

Bryant wasn't at the crime scene when I got back to the beach, but a crowd had gathered just outside the police tape. It had only been about fifteen minutes since I'd opened the gate, but these people—these adoring fans—had already created a shrine to Jess in front of one of the park rules and regulations signs. Weeping people surrounded flowers, candles, pictures, and balloons that sagged in the cold air.

I stepped into the office to find Carmen and Bryant chatting at the front counter.

"Do you see all that?" Carmen asked, popping her bubble gum. "People loved that man."

"Even if he was a big fat cheater," I said.

"Cheater in his relationship?" Carmen asked.

"And in the tournament," I said, then turned to Bryant. "Did you ever get a warrant for Jess's truck?"

Bryant nodded. "But it was empty. Not one soda bottle, candy wrapper, or anything to do with a murder."

"Damn," I said under my breath. I guess we wouldn't

be finding any evidence there. "I wonder what they did with all those coolers?"

"What coolers?" Carmen asked.

"There were several coolers in the back of Jess's truck the day of the tournament," I said. "I saw them after he'd been blown up. I'm guessing he kept various fish inside to guarantee his win."

"Do you think he did that at every competition?" Carmen asked.

"It's hard to know," I said. "But it would explain how he could always beat Molly—who was the better fisherman."

"Do you think that's why she killed him?" Carmen asked. "Because she wanted to win?"

"He'd already weighed in his fish," I said. "He still would have technically won if she hadn't caught the one at the very last minute."

"For someone with such nice taste in clothes, he sure was a dirtbag."

An idea popped into my head.

"Carmen, can you tell me anything about this video?" I pulled out my phone and showed her the footage of Molly bringing the fish in to weigh with the suspicious person in the background.

When the video finished, she shrugged. "It looked like Molly was bringing her fish to weigh, and Becca was taking something to the boat."

I glanced at Bryant, then back at Carmen. "Can you point Becca out to me?"

"Sure thing, jelly bean." She watched the short video

again and paused it when the figure in black holding the cooler came into view. "There she is. See?"

"How can you tell it's Becca?"

"She was wearing those same shoes—they're crazy expensive for tennis shoes." Carmen shrugged. "She's not wearing her fur jacket, but she probably got that out of the boat before she came up to the plaza."

As happy as I was that Molly likely wasn't the one who planted the bomb—and was highly unlikely that she had worked with Becca to do so—this was still a dead end. Literally. Becca was dead.

She couldn't tell us anything.

My head felt like it was filled with helium.

Someone else knew and had killed her to keep her quiet.

Then my balloon popped.

Molly was the one who looked like she killed Becca. And she had the bomb parts in her room.

"Why is your face doing those things?" Carmen asked.

"Because she realized she was wrong," Bryant said. "And that her friend was in on the murder."

"But why would Molly and Becca work together?" I asked. "Maybe they didn't hate each other as much as it seemed, but they certainly weren't friends." The image of Molly and Becca chatting at Becca's car popped into my head. Were they friends? If they were, Molly could have done it.

"We're working on the why, but the evidence proves Molly killed Becca," Bryant said. "Maybe they were in on the bomb plot together, and then Becca wanted to come clean."

"Molly killed someone?" Carmen shook her head. "No way. She wouldn't have."

"We found Becca dead," I said. "Molly was standing over her body covered in blood."

It was the only possible truth. Not only did this mean Molly would rot in prison, it meant I wouldn't get my three million dollars.

I almost laughed at myself.

What would I have done with three million dollars, anyway?

19

The day drug on. I wanted to be home and away from a murder scene. George was assigned to the reservoir but pretty much stayed to himself. Thankfully. I didn't know that I'd have much patience for his antics.

"Ranger Five, Ranger Seven?" Antonio's voice came through the radio.

He was working the afternoon shift and had called in service only a few minutes before.

"Go ahead," I said.

"Can you come up to the shop when you get a chance?"

I couldn't help it. My heart pounded every time Antonio asked me to meet him somewhere. There was an attraction, but that was it. We'd kissed once, and it had almost ruined everything with Garrett. I wouldn't let that happen again. But still, his voice was like warm caramel.

"I'll be right there," I said in the most serious voice I could.

The crowd had only grown around Jess's shrine since the morning. Now there were cameras from local news stations capturing the scene.

"What's up?" I asked when I walked into the shop.

Antonio was leaning up against his truck, going through some paperwork.

When he turned, he didn't have a smile on his gorgeous Italian face.

"You need to be careful," he said. "I know you have worked cases before, but there is something off about this one. Molly is in jail, but everyone knows she didn't do it. Harry is letting you help when you are not a cop—no offense—and—"

I put a hand on his arm. "It's okay," I said. "Everything will be fine."

We stood there for a moment. Then I dropped my hand to my side.

"You are getting married soon." Antonio looked past me as he spoke. "You will have a husband and eventually kids. What you are doing is dangerous. You have to think about that."

"It's not like I go looking for problems," I said, defensiveness welling up inside me. "They just seem to find me."

"I know," Antonio said. "And that is the problem." He turned away. "I just wanted to ask you to be more careful. Especially on this case."

I sighed. "I will."

I hopped into the truck and headed back down to the boat ramp parking lot to finish my shift.

When a tap at my window interrupted my thoughts, I turned to find a camera pointed right at my face.

"What are you doing?" I asked as I hopped out of my ranger truck. I only had a couple more hours before my shift was over. This was the last thing I needed. "Stop."

But the cameraman didn't stop.

"Let's film a bit, and if you don't like it, you don't have to do it." Howard smiled from behind the cameraman. I glanced around the parking lot. Where had they even come from?

"Not so fast," Wanda said, rushing over to me, her own cameraman following behind. "If Rylie signs with anyone, it will be me."

Antonio hopped out of his ranger truck and stepped between me and the cameras. "Rylie is not signing with anyone. She asked you to stop."

The cameramen dropped their cameras.

"Now, you can each speak with Rylie," Antonio said. "With the cameras off. If she is willing to speak with you."

"I think I need to talk to Detective Bryant first," I said. "Do you see him?"

Antonio looked around. "Maybe he left. I will call him on his cell. Are you okay?"

I nodded. "Yeah," I said. "I'm good."

He gave both Wanda and Howard a glare before walking back to his truck, his cell phone to his ear.

"How about this?" Howard said, interrupting my thoughts. "We'll each pitch you an idea, and you can choose which one you like best."

"I don't want to be on TV," I said. "I'm perfectly fine being a plain old park ranger."

"There's nothing plain about you being a park ranger," Ursula said, coming up from behind me. "If there's anything I know, you're the most interesting park ranger we've ever had and possibly the most interesting in the country."

"Why? Because I seem to stumble across dead bodies everywhere I go?" I asked. "I would call that depressing over interesting."

"I think this would be a good opportunity for both you and the city," Ursula muttered so only I could hear. "Let's listen to their proposals."

I needed to find a murderer. Not listen to pitches about reality TV.

"You can still be a park ranger," Wanda said. "We don't want you to change anything you do. No faking necessary." She shot a glare at Howard, who looked like he might stick his tongue out at her.

"We don't fake things," Howard said. "But what's reality TV without a bit of drama."

If I signed with anyone, it would be Wanda. At least she cared about Molly. Howard didn't seem to care at all that two people under his employ had recently died.

"Fine," I said. "I'll listen. But no promises."

All three nodded excitedly—Ursula most of all.

We headed to the banquet hall, where each of them basically went over the same proposals—a day in the life of a real-life park ranger complete with all the incidences that came with being a total shit magnet.

Ursula was so close to the edge, she looked like she might fall out of her seat. I—on the other hand—was not.

Nothing they said made me want to be on TV. In fact, their pitches had the opposite effect.

"Do you have any questions for us?" Wanda asked when they were finished.

I thought for a minute, then smiled. "Do either of you know who killed Jess and Becca?"

The room went silent. Three gaping mouths stared at me.

"Because I know it wasn't Molly, and I feel like there's something that the two of you might know that you're not telling the police. Something that could end this entire investigation."

I was reaching. Howard had nothing to gain from Jess and Becca's deaths. Wanda could have been snuffing out the competition, but I doubted it.

Neither spoke. Neither moved. The room was a ball of tension.

Until Ursula laughed. "She doesn't mean that."

It was my turn to gape at her. "I do mean that." I turned back to the two producers. "Look, I know Jess was cheating. I know you helped him." I pointed at Howard. "I know Becca had the cooler with the bomb. I don't believe Becca acted alone, but I know she and Molly weren't in cahoots. That leaves someone who isn't giving us the entire story. Someone who wanted Jess dead. And when Becca threatened to come clean to the police, that someone killed her too."

I sat there and waited. Silence once again overtook the room.

"That's absurd," Wanda finally said. "Why would Becca want Jess dead?"

"Exactly," Howard said. "She may not have shown it, but when she and I were—you know—she called out his name. She loved him."

"You slept with her? After he died?" Wanda looked like she might smack Howard. "You are the lowest of lows. You know that, right?"

"A man has needs," he said. "If you'd have known that, we might still be together."

Ursula and I exchanged a look. What had I started?

"I most certainly did know that," Wanda said. "But your needs could never be met. Never. You were insatiable. And now you're sleeping with a girl half your age whose fiancé just died? I thought you had *some* standards."

"I was with you." Howard laughed. "My standards went out the window a long time ago."

This time, Wanda did deck him. He flew out of his chair, blood spurting from his nose.

"What the hell is wrong with you?" he screamed.

"You deserved that. And so much more," Wanda said, then turned to me. "Think about my offer and let me know."

20

"That sounds interesting," Garrett said when we sat down for dinner that night. He'd made steak and potatoes. "You would be fantastic on TV."

I frowned. I was certain he'd be on my side. "But it's so intrusive."

"You would get paid twice to do the same job," he said. "That sounds like good financial sense."

He was an accountant—it was understandable why he'd see it that way.

"But I'm not good on TV," I said. "You saw my YouTube video."

"That's part of the reason I fell in love with you."

"I killed a little girl's sandcastle."

"And wrestled a snake."

"Before it bit me, and I thought I was going to die."

He laughed. "Okay, but that was unsuspected."

"I don't know." My certainty about not doing the show was crumbling. If Garrett thought it was a good idea, why wouldn't I do it?

"It's your call," he said. "I'll support whatever you decide. But think of the kind of house we could raise our kids in if you were a television star."

"Heck, if I would have figured out who the murderer was by the end of tonight, I would have made three million dollars."

He sucked in a breath, and his eyes widened. He dropped his fork and knife on the plate with a clatter and grabbed at his neck.

"Oh my God," I said. "Are you choking?"

He nodded, panic setting into his eyes.

I'd given the Heimlich a million times. It was nothing for me to wrap my arms around his toned waist and thrust my fists upward.

But the piece of steak he'd inhaled was lodged in there good.

"I'm so sorry," I said as I tried over and over again to get it dislodged. "Stay with me. I'll get it."

His arms flopped at his sides as I pulled up under his ribs as hard as I could.

Nothing.

He needed to cough. Needed to breathe.

I gave him a few back blows and then went back to the Heimlich.

Then he went limp.

"Dammit." I could have called an ambulance, but they wouldn't have been there in time. This was up to me.

I laid him on his back and checked in his mouth for the piece of steak.

There was no steak. He wasn't breathing.

I gave two rescue breaths. They wouldn't go in.

Tears streaked down my face. I brushed them away before I started compressions.

One, two, three—I thrust my weight down onto his chest.

Nothing.

I kept going. He couldn't die. Not from a piece of steak.

Twenty-five, twenty-six, twenty-seven—

Garrett folded in half and rolled toward me, the piece of steak dropping onto the floor by my knee.

He gasped for air, and I threw myself on top of him. "Oh, thank God, you're okay."

"You're my hero," he whispered.

We stayed there on the floor for a long time until he said, "Now, what do we need to do to get you that three million dollars?"

It didn't take long to get Garrett up to speed on the investigation. It was the first time he seemed interested in one of the investigations I was working on.

"So, you think someone was working with Becca, and then Becca wanted to come clean, but this person didn't, so they killed her?" Garrett asked.

"Basically," I said.

"But what if she killed Jess so she could get the show, and then her ex-boyfriend killed her? Isn't he the one who tipped you off Molly would be there? Maybe he called Molly and told her to go to Becca's room just in time for you to find Molly with Becca's dead body."

"I thought that might be the case too," I said. "I'm impressed. Maybe you should become a cop."

"I don't think they let guys with convicted felon brothers be cops," he said. His twin brother had been in cahoots with some pretty bad people a while back. People who killed other people. He was in prison now.

"So what do we need to do to get a confession from this guy?" Garrett said.

I had no idea he would be so motivated by the idea of money. I mean, sure, three million dollars was pretty awesome, but for us to figure out who murdered Becca and Jess in the span of a few hours would be nearly impossible.

"I guess we need to find him first," I said. "I don't know how, but—"

"I'll make some calls," Garrett said.

Garrett had never been sexier. Not only was he physically sexy in his faded jeans and tight t-shirt, but the thought of him helping me investigate a case was a huge turn-on.

My phone chimed in my pocket with a text.

It was Luke.

I hear you're going to be a big TV star.

I texted back.

Who told you?

Shayla.

Well, it's not a for sure thing.

Why not?

I don't know if I want to be on TV.

You'd be great. But I understand. It would be a lot of pressure.

And money.

That would be nice.

I sighed.

"I managed to get through to Bobby's room at the hotel," Garrett said. "He agreed to meet us in an hour."

I glanced down at my phone and turned it off.

"Everything okay?" he asked, glancing from me to my phone and back to me again.

"It's Luke," I said. "Shayla told him I might do a TV program."

"Let me guess—he thinks it's a bad idea." Garrett smiled.

"No," I said. "He didn't say either way."

Garrett didn't respond.

Forty-five minutes later, we were in the car pulling up to the hotel.

"Do you want me to talk at all?" Garrett asked.

"If you want to," I said. "This was your idea, after all."

He smiled. I knew the rush he was feeling. The first time I'd interviewed someone of interest on a case, I felt it too.

Bobby looked anxious when we walked in.

"Look, the police already talked to me," he said before we could even sit down. "I didn't hurt Becca."

"We're just here to talk," Garrett said, taking the lead. "Why don't we sit down and have a drink?"

Bobby hesitated, then sat. "I don't drink—been sober five years," Bobby said. "But I'd take a water."

Garrett ordered the two of us beers and a water for Bobby.

When the waitress walked away, Garrett started, "Why were you following my girlfriend on her run?"

"Uh—I—" Bobby stammered.

"Garrett," I said. "What does that have to do—"

"Were you going to kill her too?" Garrett demanded, slamming a fist on the table.

Maybe he wasn't cut out for this.

"I didn't kill anyone," Bobby said, glancing around to make sure no one was listening. The bar was empty besides a couple of bartenders. "I wanted to tell her about Becca's tendency to make bombs."

"Sure you did," Garrett said.

Maybe we should have gone over proper questioning techniques before we came in. I had a feeling this would get us nowhere.

I put a hand on Garrett's arm, but he didn't stop.

"You threatened to kill Becca if she didn't kill Jess, then killed her after she did because she was going to turn you into the cops, isn't that right?" Garrett sucked in a breath and looked like he might keep going until the waitress showed up.

"Is everything okay over here?" she said with a smile in her voice. Then her smile vanished when she noticed the epic stare-down happening between Bobby and Garrett.

I took the drinks and set them on the table in front of us. "Thank you," I said, handing her cash.

"You have it all wrong," Bobby said through gritted

teeth. "I thought you came here to hear my side of the story? Not to accuse me of killing people."

"We did," I said before Garrett could say anything else. "Why don't you tell us your side of the story?"

"I loved Becca."

"Enough to kill Jess for?" Garrett said.

I felt my eyes almost pop out of their sockets.

I knew he wanted to get that money, but badgering this guy wouldn't get us there.

"I. Didn't. Kill. Jess." Bobby said. "And if you say I did again, I'm out of here."

I was surprised he hadn't left yet.

"Go on," I said. "Keep telling us your story."

"Becca and Jess were never good together. It was only a publicity stunt. When Jess died, sure, I thought maybe she and I would have a chance. But then I saw her cozying up with that producer. I realized then that she probably killed Jess to get him out of the way so she could have the show."

"So you killed her," Garrett said.

Bobby let out a mix between a growl and a yell, stood up, and flipped the table over, spilling our drinks all over us.

I slid back and jumped out of my chair, but it was too late. I was covered in water and beer.

"I didn't kill anyone! Even if Becca was alive, we'd still be done! Forever!" Bobby turned and stormed out of the bar.

Garrett looked at me with an oblivious smile. "I think that went well. Now we just need to tell the police."

21

The time expired.

I would not be a millionaire.

But that was okay. I'd learned a valuable lesson: don't let Garrett investigate murders. In fact, I intended to keep him as far away from investigations as possible.

He had already gone to work when I woke up the next morning. As bad as I felt, it was nice not to have to rehash the night before.

It took almost everything I had to convince Garrett that we had absolutely nothing to tell the police. He'd recorded the entire conversation with this phone, which was a good idea, but the conversation had yielded nothing.

Did Garrett's theory hold water?

Sure.

But there was no evidence Bobby had anything to do with either death.

When Molly called, I was ready to throw in the towel.

"They figured out who did it," Molly said. "And they said it was you who gave them the information."

"What are you talking about?" I asked. "I haven't even spoken with the police."

"Well, Detective Bryant told me you're the one who got me released."

"I didn't," I said. "He's probably trying to get me the money you and Wanda promised."

"You didn't talk to Bobby last night?"

"I did but—"

"And did he admit to the murders?"

I scratched Fizzy's head. "No, he denied the murders."

"But he left a note saying—"

"Wait," I said. "He left a note?"

"He shot himself last night," Molly said. "His note confessed everything."

I stood up, and before I knew it, I was putting on my shoes. "No," I said. "He couldn't have."

"I guess that means you're a millionaire," she said, a smile in her voice.

"Keep your money. It's not true."

"But—"

"Bobby didn't kill Becca and Jess."

"He tried to set me up," she said. "If he didn't do it, the cops will still think I did."

I was stuck.

I knew Bobby didn't kill anyone. At least I felt like he hadn't. But maybe it was an act. "Did they find the gun?"

"I think so," Molly said. "I don't know. You'll have to talk to the police. But aren't you happy?"

"No," I said. "I don't want money I didn't earn—

money that might have caused someone to end his own life."

"Oh." Her voice turned more somber. "I hadn't thought of it that way."

"I have to talk to the police," I said. "I'll call you later."

We disconnected, and I immediately dialed Bryant.

"Bryant," he said on the first ring. He probably hadn't even looked at the caller ID.

"It's Rylie," I said. "Bobby didn't kill anyone."

Bryant took a deep breath and then said, "How can you be so sure? He left a note. A detailed note. How would he have gotten the information about the crime if he didn't do it?"

"Because the person who did do it is setting him up to take the fall," I said. "Can I come to the crime scene?"

Bryant sighed. "Fine, but no touching anything."

I got dressed faster than I had since I was a senior in high school and wanted to sleep in until the very last minute before going to school.

The hotel Bobby stayed at looked different than it had the night before. Where there was practically no one, now people swarmed the lobby. Police stood at the stairs and the elevators, only letting certain people go upstairs.

I was one of them.

When I got to Bobby's hotel room, the body had been taken away, but blood and other items were still there.

Actually, it looked like he'd had a party. Beer cans littered the still-made bed and surrounding floor. An empty bottle of whiskey sat on the table next to a glass half filled with booze.

"What do you see?" Bryant asked.

I looked around more closely. The last time someone had asked me that, it was Seamus, and we'd each seen something completely different on the other side of binoculars. In that case, I'd been right. But Bryant was a trained detective. He wouldn't be easy to out-observe.

"There are beer cans and whiskey bottles, but Bobby didn't drink. He was sober five years," I said. "Maybe he fell off the wagon one last time. Or maybe someone else was here." I glanced over at Bryant, who motioned for me to go on.

"The shot happened here," I pointed to where blood stained the wall and carpet. "He was standing but fell. And the note? Where's the note?"

"They took it to get fingerprints," Bryant said. "But I'm almost certain they'll be Bobby's."

I walked around the room a bit more. The blankets on the bed were flattened in the shape of a butt and legs. Bobby was probably sitting up watching TV.

"Can I touch this?" I asked, pointing to the remote.

Bryant handed me a glove.

I turned on the TV. It was paused on an action movie. When I pushed play, the TV roared, making everyone in the room cover their ears. I clicked it off quickly. "Maybe someone was trying to mask the sound of a confrontation," I said. "Have you talked to the neighbors?"

"The surrounding rooms are empty."

"Can you tell me what the note said?" I looked around for more clues. Anything.

"Bobby admitted to killing Becca and Jess in great detail. He also said now he'd be able to be with his forever love in the next life."

"He called her his forever love?" I asked. "Because when we left him, he seemed pretty done with her."

Bryant looked at me as if I was grasping at straws.

"I have a recording of our conversation with him last night," I said. Garrett had insisted on sending it to me the minute we got in the car so I could share it with the police. I hadn't intended on doing so since it made Garrett look bad, but maybe it would convince Bryant that Bobby hadn't done this.

"Maybe he came back here, turned on the TV, and started contemplating what he'd done," Bryant said. "Maybe he got drunk and ended it all."

I shrugged. "Or maybe someone else did this. Just like someone tried to set Molly up."

"But who?" Bryant asked.

"Well, we've been through everyone but Wanda and Howard," I said. "Unless it was some crazy fan or someone related to Becca."

"Becca doesn't have many relationships outside of the show and the wrestling arena."

"Another wrestler, then?" I asked.

"There was an event this weekend." Bryant shook his head. "Bobby and Becca skipped it."

I was trying to come up with another explanation when my phone chimed in my pocket.

Dammit. I'd forgotten all about the wedding dress shopping appointment my mom had set up for today.

"I'll talk to you later. I have a wedding dress to find."

Bryant laughed. "Good luck."

2 2

I was tired of futzing with dresses. The minute I walked in, I went straight to the section with the lace dresses and took a deep breath. The air smelled of roses and baby powder. The boutique wasn't huge, but it was big enough for my mom, my sister, Shayla, Nikki, and Victoria to sit comfortably outside the dressing room.

We'd decided to try a different one, even though the guy who'd designed Molly's dress had practically begged us to come back. I didn't need any more bad luck.

"Lace?" Mom asked. "I thought you said no lace."

I shrugged. "Maybe I need to at least try some with lace. Maybe it's what I've been missing." Dresses with lace were the only dresses I hadn't tried. And maybe that was the problem. Maybe I needed to find a lace one since that's what Garrett wanted. It was both our wedding, after all.

"Whatever you say," Mom said and helped me to the dressing room with the four gowns I'd haphazardly chosen from the rack that had some sort of lace on them.

The first made everyone's noses wrinkle. It didn't fit right and made me look like a linebacker.

"The dresses can be altered to fit, of course," the shop owner said in her cheery voice.

Nikki shook her head. "Next."

I traded one for another and then another and another. I was starting to think I'd need to go back to the drawing board when I put on the last one.

I glanced in the mirror before walking out. It was a v-neck, with a lace back and white buttons all the way down. It was exactly what Garrett wanted. And it didn't look terrible on me. Was it what I would have chosen for myself? Who knows? I hadn't had any luck up until now. And between the two of us, Garrett was definitely the more stylish one.

I sucked in a breath and put on a smile before opening the door to the faces of the women I loved most in the world.

They were speechless.

It wasn't until they each cracked a smile that I realized their silence meant they liked it.

"I think this is the one," I said, butterflies rising in my chest, making it hard to breathe.

"It's beautiful," Mom said.

"It really is," Shayla said. "Not what I thought you'd choose, but it is beautiful."

I thought I heard Nikki mutter, "Finally," under her breath.

I turned to see my profile in the mirror. Not bad. I still needed to lose about ten more pounds and do about four million sit-ups so my stomach wouldn't bulge out. But it didn't look awful at all.

"We can make any adjustments you need," the saleslady said, but her voice sounded like it was coming from very far away. "Alterations are included in the price."

"If you don't mind me asking, how much is it?" My mom asked. It wasn't like she put a spending limit on the dress—she and Dad had plenty of money and had balked at Garrett's offer to help pay for the wedding—but I'd decided early on I didn't want to take advantage of their generosity.

"It's forty-five hundred."

The numbers swirled in my head, making me feel faint. Forty-five hundred dollars? More than four *thousand* dollars?

"Rylie, do not faint again," Mom said. "It's perfectly okay."

I sucked in a breath and steadied myself on a chair. "I can't," I said. "I'll find something else."

"No," Mom said. "If this means we never have to step foot in a bridal boutique again—no offense—" she said to the saleslady "—then I'd pay forty million."

"So would I," Nikki mumbled.

We all laughed.

I glanced in the mirror one more time.

This was it.

The dress I would get married in.

"I still can't believe you almost passed out when she told us how much it cost." Victoria sat next to me at one of my favorite Italian restaurants. Mom figured she'd take us all out for a celebratory lunch. The rest of the women sat around the circular table, throwing random worried glances in my direction.

"I didn't know dresses could cost that much," I said. "I mean, I did, but not for me."

"My dress cost more than that," Megan—my sister—said.

"But yours was handmade to be what you wanted," I said.

"The price is perfectly acceptable." Mom smiled at me. "Now, we have to finalize the rest of the wedding plans. What else is there to do?"

"Nothing," I said. "Garrett and I have settled everything."

"And then both of my babies will finally be married," Mom said. "I was starting to worry you'd become a lonely cat lady who lived in the forest and looked for dead bodies all the time."

She laughed, but I knew there was a touch of honesty in what she had to say.

"Speaking of dead bodies," I said. "There's another one."

"Bobby," Victoria said. "We heard."

Shayla didn't say anything but nodded along with Nikki.

"It's sad that he killed the other two and then himself," Mom said. "What a tragic existence."

"But that's the thing," I said. "I don't think he did."

Shayla's eyes widened as she looked up from her water glass. "What do you mean, you don't think he did?"

"I don't think he killed himself, and I don't think he killed anyone else."

"But the evidence is all there," Shayla said, then glanced around as if she'd said something that might have gotten her fired. "I can't discuss this with you, but it's over. You can rest assured."

The waiter arrived with our food, interrupting the conversation. Shayla's baked ziti looked delicious, making my salad—though beautifully plated—look like a giant pile of rabbit food. Oh well, it was only a few more weeks, and I'd be able to go back to eating normally.

"What made you decide to go with lace?" Nikki asked, taking a swig of her wine and changing the subject from the murder investigation.

"It was actually something Garrett mentioned," I said. "When I asked him what he thought I should wear, he said he liked lace."

Nikki narrowed her eyes at me. "But you hate lace."

"Hate is a strong word," I said. The dress had looked better on me than I imagined lace would. "Plus, I hadn't given it a chance until today."

Nikki didn't look appeased by this answer but let it go. It wasn't her wedding. Maybe when she got married, she'd understand the concept of compromise.

"It's not what I expected," Mom said. "But you looked breathtaking. Your mountain wedding will be perfect."

I smiled. I'd finally found the dress. Now if I could just figure out who planted that bomb.

"I found a dress," I said when I walked into Garrett's. "And I think you'll like it."

Babbitt and Fizzy both ran to me for their nightly welcome loves. Since I spent almost every night at Garrett's, Fizzy just stayed there and kept Babbitt company during the days.

I bent down and kissed Garrett.

"Lace?" Garrett asked.

"I'll never tell," I said.

"Did you hear about Bobby?" Garrett frowned.

I'd hoped he hadn't heard about Bobby, but the news had been following the story very closely.

"I guess you were right," I said. I'd tried to accept that the police were right. Bobby had done it. And then offed himself.

"I don't like being right," Garrett said. "Do you think he killed himself because of me?"

I shook my head. "No," I said. "I think he was plagued with guilt. He probably would have done it either way."

"I don't think I'll be playing bad cop—or good cop, for that matter—for a long time. Investigative work is not for me."

I sat next to him on the couch and snuggled into him. "That's okay. It's not for everyone."

"Did you decide to do the TV show?"

I shook my head. "I haven't thought about it much."

"You don't have to do it if you don't want to, but I do think you'd do well at it."

It was nice having his support and encouragement.

"I'm pretty beat," I said. "I think I'll head to bed. I have to work early tomorrow."

"Sounds good," Garrett said. "I'll be up in a while."

I took a shower and put on my PJs. My phone rang with a video call the minute I was tucked into bed.

It was Luke.

I went back and forth. It's not that I didn't want to talk to him. I did. But I was starting to think it wasn't the best thing for my relationship with Garrett.

I silenced the phone and put it on the nightstand before turning off the light and falling dead asleep.

When I awoke, I was disoriented. Garrett wasn't in bed. The sun wasn't out. But I felt like I'd slept an entire night.

I checked the time.

It was two in the morning.

Usually, Garrett wasn't that late.

I rushed downstairs, panicked.

What if something had happened to him?

Babbitt and Fizzy were asleep on the floor at the bottom of the stairs and didn't even lift their heads when I ran past.

"Garrett?" I called out.

But when I got to the living room, I found him. Asleep.

My heart felt like it might shatter.

Why had my mind instantly gone to something bad happening? Why hadn't I assumed he probably fell asleep?

Maybe I needed to stop investigating these crimes. They were starting to affect my sleep, my relationships, my life.

"Hey babe," I said, rubbing Garrett's shoulder, but he didn't wake up. "Garrett?" I shook him harder, but nothing.

I could see his chest rise and fall, but he wouldn't gain consciousness.

"He's not going to wake up," a voice said behind me.

I turned to find Howard standing in the doorway to the kitchen. He was holding an empty syringe and a glass of whiskey.

"What do you mean he won't wake up?"

"Not unless you come with me." He opened the door to the garage. "I drugged the dogs too."

My mind went back to Fizzy and Babbitt lying together at the bottom of the stairs. "If anything happens to them, I'll rip you limb from limb."

"It's interesting you have such a different reaction to me drugging your fiancé versus me drugging your dogs."

I could feel the tears building in my throat. I'd left my phone on the nightstand upstairs. Garrett's was probably in his pocket.

I had no way to contact anyone. To call for help.

"I'm not going anywhere with you."

He set an almost-finished glass of whiskey on the counter and pulled a gun from the back of his waistband.

"Yes, you are." He pointed it at me, his finger on the trigger.

"How many guns do you have?" I asked.

"I have as many guns as I need," he said. "I have unlimited resources. I can do whatever I want."

"Like kill a bunch of people?" I asked. "How many more will you kill? Me? Garrett? The police will catch you."

He laughed. "If they do, I'll get off easy. I have good attorneys."

I glanced around to find something I could use against him. By the way he swayed, I'd guess he'd had quite a lot to drink before I came downstairs.

"Don't get smart, missy. You had your chance to play nice. I offered you your own television show. You didn't have to investigate this murder. Now, you've put me in a position I can't let you out of."

"If you're going to kill me, why would I go with you?" I asked, stalling. "Just kill me here."

"Because if you go with me, I'll let your fiancé and—more importantly—your doggies live."

Well then.

I followed him out to the garage and then out into the driveway.

"Get in the back," he said.

When I opened the door on the passenger side, I found Molly lying across the seat, passed out.

"You didn't kill Molly," I said.

"Not yet." He nudged me with the gun. "Get in."

I slid inside, lifting Molly and moving her over to rest against her window.

"Give me your hands."

I held my hands out, and he put a zip tie around them at the wrists. I nearly cried in relief. I'd be able to get free when the time was right. I only hoped I'd be able to stay alive long enough to thank George for teaching me and Logan for making me practice.

When Howard slammed the door, I immediately tried to open it, but he'd put the child locks on. I couldn't get out unless I crawled over the seats. But Molly was in the way. And my hands were tied together.

I checked for a pulse. It was still there. She was also breathing. I guess whatever he'd given Garrett and the dogs, he'd given her too.

"Why didn't you drug me?" I asked when he slid into the driver's seat. "I was asleep. I probably wouldn't have even noticed."

"If you hadn't noticed, I'm a bit wasted." He started the car and sped off, hitting a mailbox on his way. "I could have never gotten you down the stairs and out to the car in my condition. You're not exactly light like little miss Mollykins."

Ouch.

"That's what that idiot always called her. Jess's little Mollykins." He made a gagging sound. "It was disgusting."

"Why did you kill him? He made you so much money."

"I didn't kill him," he said. "Becca did. And she wasn't supposed to. She was supposed to keep him away from the boat. The explosion was supposed to be for dramatic effect. No one else was around. It would have been perfect. But she let him get blown up, the bimbo."

"So, naturally, you had to kill her."

"Naturally." He shrugged. "Then Bobby got wind of it. Probably from you."

"I didn't tell Bobby anything," I said. "I had no idea it was you."

"Right." He looked at me in the rearview mirror. "You must think I'm a complete and total dumbass. I might be crazy, but I could see how you looked at me with those suspicious eyes."

"So, what's your plan?" I asked.

He swerved into oncoming traffic. I held my breath as headlights charged at us.

A horn honked, and he jerked the wheel, sending the car back into our lane just in time.

"Whoa, whoa," he said. "Don't go killing all of us."

He was talking to himself.

He drove faster than any human being should sober. If his gun didn't end up killing us, his car would.

"Gabe?" Molly said as she began to regain consciousness.

"Molly, it's okay," I said through tears.

"It's not okay," Howard said. "It's not going to be okay."

"Oh my God," Molly said. "I thought it was a dream. Where's Gabe?"

"He's right where you left him," Howard said.

"Is he alive?" she whispered.

"For now," he said. "And he'll stay alive if you do what I tell you to."

"What's that?"

"Spoiler alert." He laughed to himself. "You like fishing so much, I thought you might like to do a little swimming."

"You're going to drown us?" I asked.

"I'm going to drown her," he said. "Or rather, you're going to drown her."

"And what will you do with me?" I asked.

"You'll meet the same fate as dear old Bobby."

"You're insane," Molly said.

"Not insane," he replied. "Smart."

"Do you have a plan?" Molly whispered to me.

I shook my head.

"Now, now." He turned all the way around in his seat, not caring that he was veering all over the road. "No secrets." He waved the gun in our faces. "Or else."

He pulled the trigger, and the bullet went right between us, shattering the back window.

Molly and I both screamed.

Howard laughed.

That was it.

If I was going to die one way or another, I would go down with a fight.

"Hold on," I whispered to Molly.

She grabbed the door handle and nodded.

The reservoir entry was just up ahead. He'd have to slow down a bit to make the turn. Otherwise, we'd end up in a field.

And when he made the turn, I'd make my move.

Sure enough, he started to slow, and when we were in the middle of the turn, I pulled my legs up into a ball and then kicked them out at his head, smashing him into his driver's side door.

His head hit the window with a deafening crack.

Howard was unconscious, but the car was speeding toward the gate.

There was nothing I could do to stop us.

I pulled my legs back under me in the back seat, raised my hands, and yanked them down, breaking the zip ties.

Just before we hit the gate, I launched myself between the two front seats, grabbed the steering wheel, and yanked it to the side.

We skidded sideways, and the driver's side of the car plowed into the gate. If the gate hadn't been as tall as it was, we probably would have rolled over it, but it held firm.

"Molly, are you okay?" I asked.

She gave me a groggy yes.

I crawled into the front seat and took the gun before opening the passenger door and getting out of the car.

I let Molly out the back, helped her out of her zip ties, and then went back into the passenger seat to see if Howard was still alive.

He had a pulse but was losing a lot of blood.

"That son of a monkey's butt can't die," Molly said.

"Let me in. I'll put pressure on his wounds. He needs to go to prison for the things he's done."

"Agreed," I said, getting out and letting her in. "But I don't know that we'll be able to keep him alive before someone finds us. It's the middle of the night, and I don't have a phone. Do you?"

"Nope," she said. "Maybe he does."

Molly pressed her scarf to his head while I searched the car.

No phone.

I moved to the trunk, but still nothing.

"Now, what are we going to do?"

"You're going to die," Howard grunted.

Molly fell backward out of the car onto her butt.

"No, please don't shoot me," Molly said, crab-crawling backward.

"You should have killed me when you had the chance," Howard said, pointing his gun at a defenseless Molly.

Then the gunshot rang out.

"No!" I jumped into the back seat to tackle Howard, but he had gone limp.

When I looked out the window, George was standing with a gun in his hand.

Tatiana had thrown herself over Molly.

And Sondra had a phone in her hand, talking to who I assumed would be the police.

Tatiana helped a sobbing Molly up.

I jumped out of the car. "What are you all doing here?"

"Saving your ass," George said. "I knew something was up with this guy."

His I-told-you-so tone of voice didn't even bother me. In fact, I had the overwhelming urge to hug him.

"How did you know we'd be here?" Molly asked.

"Ursula told us to keep an eye on you," Tatiana said to me. "Did you really think we were hired to simply be summer park rangers?"

Sondra rolled her eyes behind George, still talking into the phone.

"We followed you from Garrett's house," he said. "He lost us a bit back there, but I caught up. And just in time. Why didn't you shoot him?"

"He was passed out," I said. "I didn't know he had another gun."

"Have you not been listening to me at all?" George said. "Never assume they only have one weapon. And if they're passed out, always check for weapons."

"Noted," I said. "Now, we need to get back to Gabe and Garrett and Babbitt and Fizzy."

"The cops are already at Garrett's," Sondra said. "Where is Gabe? I'll have them go there too."

"My hotel room," Molly said. I thought I could almost see a blush rise in her cheeks when she said it.

Flashing lights came up the road behind us.

Bryant stepped out almost before the car stopped moving. "What the hell happened here?"

"It was Howard," I said. "He did all of it."

Bryant reached out and put an arm around my shoulder, to which I turned in and accepted a full-on hug. With the adrenaline wearing off, the tears came.

"I'm sorry I didn't believe you," he said. "I should have listened."

"Yeah, you should have," I said between sobs.

"Come on, let's get you home," Bryant said and led us to his police cruiser. "Good work, you three," he said to a smiling George, Tatiana, and Sondra. "I thought it might have been a bit of overkill hiring the three of you to protect Rylie and her shit magnet tendencies, but apparently Ursula knew what she was doing."

Gabe, Garrett, Babbit, and Fizzy were all okay. They were groggy for a while—especially the dogs—but it seemed like Howard had been telling the truth that he wasn't going to kill them.

Guilt was a persistent feeling as the week went on. Every part of me knew this was my fault. I could hardly look Garrett in the eye.

I stayed at Shayla's and my apartment and kept to myself in bed. Everyone had given me space. Ursula gave me time off. I spent a week in bed cuddled up with Fizzy while I wept at the thought of being the reason people and pups may have died.

When my phone rang for the fourteenth time in one day—every call from Luke—I finally answered.

"Hello?" My voice was scratchy. I hadn't used it in so long.

"I hear you've become a hermit."

"Maybe." I pulled my blankets up higher toward my face.

"Why?"

"It doesn't matter," I said. "I'm fine."

"You need to let Garrett in," Luke said. "He's your fiancé."

"I almost got him killed," I said. "He almost died because of me."

"You didn't almost get him killed," Luke said. "You cannot take the blame for a psychopath's actions."

"If I hadn't been investigating, none of this would have happened."

"As much as I hate to say this, you're right," Luke said. "But if you hadn't been persistent—at least from what Detective Bryant said—that Howard guy would still be out there. Dangerous. And ready to kill again."

I didn't respond.

"Sometimes, in this line of work, you have to know things will get hairy. Things could be dangerous."

"I'm not a cop, Luke," I said. "I'm a park ranger. I didn't ask for any of this. I don't know why it follows me. But I'm done. I don't want it anymore. If this is what being a park ranger is, I quit."

"You can't quit, Rylie," Luke's voice was kind, caring. And it made me want to punch him in the face. He was halfway around the world. He didn't get to have a say in my life.

"You know what? I'm quitting. And I think I need to go. I need to wash my hair."

Luke sighed. "Don't do something you'll regret. I know they love having you out there."

"Okay, thanks for your advice. I hope you're having fun doing whatever it is you're doing in Timbuktu." I couldn't keep the pain out of my voice. I was still hurt that he'd abandoned me. He'd decided we couldn't be a couple, and that was fine, but what was wrong with being my friend? He could have been with me in person, talking to me in my room instead of from across the globe.

"Take care of yourself, Rylie," he said.

"You too," I said and hung up the phone.

2 7

Garrett came over that evening. He made dinner while I showered, and then we turned on a favorite TV show and snuggled on the couch.

Any time I tried to tell him I was sorry, he stopped me. He told me the same thing Luke had. It wasn't my fault. Blah, blah, blah.

But it was. And I had to do something about it.

"I'm going to quit my job as a park ranger," I said when a commercial came on.

"Tell me more about that," Garrett said.

"I'm tired of putting you in danger. Putting myself in danger. Putting everyone I love in danger."

"Rylie, this is not your fault. I don't know how many times I have to tell you that. I'm not angry, and I don't want you to quit."

I sat in silence.

"That being said," he continued, "if you want to quit, I stand behind you. I'm here for you, no matter what."

"Even if I'm unemployed?"

"I can take care of both of us," he said. "But I think you'll be bored."

He was right. Eventually, I would get bored. "I'll get a job," I said. "I just don't know what."

"That's okay," he said. "And if you want to stay being a ranger, you can do that."

I shook my head. I'd made my decision. There was no part of me that wanted to put the uniform back on. No part of me that wanted to see Garrett passed out on the couch and worry about his safety.

I wanted a normal life.

"I'll call Ursula tomorrow."

"If that's what you want to do," he said.

"It is."

"Hey, Ursula, this is Rylie," I said on the phone the next day.

"Hey," she said. "You calling to tell me you're coming back to work?"

"Not exactly," I said.

"I figured as much." She sighed. "Rylie, I know why you're calling, and I can't say I blame you. But I also think this is a brash decision. One that you might regret."

I was already nervous to talk to her. I didn't consider the possibility that she'd try to convince me to stay.

"I don't think I can do it anymore," I said, my voice cracking.

"How about this," she said. "The city will pay for counseling. You've been through a lot. And then, after your wedding, we can revisit the idea of you coming back. I won't hold my breath, but I also won't fill your position. The others can handle it without you for a month or so."

I was so set on quitting I knew my mind wouldn't change, but this seemed to be a rational agreement.

"And if I don't come back?"

"You'll always be welcome with open arms." Ursula sounded a bit choked up herself. "I'm so sorry you've been through so much during your time with us. If I could change it, I would."

I smiled. "Thank you, Ursula."

"I hope to have you back soon," she said. "Have a wonderful wedding."

She disconnected, and I leaned back on the couch with a sigh.

Everything would be okay.

Thank you so much for reading *Bungled*!

Don't miss the last book in the Rylie Cooper Series —*Snowed*—releasing October 12, 2021. Pre-order your copy today.

Can't wait for October? Check out my Magical Mane Mystery series or check out my FREE Magical Mane Mystery short story, *Meeting Mona*!

. . .

I would be honored and eternally grateful if you would post a review on Amazon and/or Goodreads about the book.

Also, I love hearing from readers! Email me at stellabixbyauthor@gmail.com.

XOXO,

Stella Bixby

ACKNOWLEDGMENTS

First of all, I want to thank God. This year has been a challenge, but without the hope and strength You've given me, it would have been so much worse.

A huge thanks to my family—all of you. You are incredibly supportive and encouraging.

Thank you to my beta readers and my ARC team. You guys are the best. I can't thank you enough for all your help!

A big thank you to my TikTok peeps. Especially, @dutchintheusa for teaching me (and Rylie) how to get out of zip ties. It might hurt, but it works! (Yes, I tried.)

And finally, thank you readers. Your emails, reviews, and comments make coming back to the keyboard so rewarding!

ABOUT THE AUTHOR

Stella Bixby is a native Coloradan who loves to snow-board, pluck at the guitar, and play board games with her family. She was once a volunteer firefighter and a park ranger, but now spends most of her time making up stories and trying to figure out what to cook for dinner.

Connect with Stella on Facebook, Twitter, and Instagram @StellaBixby.

Stella loves to hear from her readers!
www.stellabixby.com